Samuel French Acting Edition

And Then I Wrote...

by Mel Buttorff & Jack Sharkey

I0591828

‖SAMUEL FRENCH‖

SAMUELFRENCH.COM   **SAMUELFRENCH.CO.UK**

FOR PRODUCTION ENQUIRIES

UNITED STATES AND CANADA
Info@SamuelFrench.com
1-866-598-8449

UNITED KINGDOM AND EUROPE
Plays@SamuelFrench.co.uk
020-7255-4302

Each title is subject to availability from Samuel French, depending upon
country of performance. Please be aware that *AND THEN I WROTE...*
may not be licensed by Samuel French in your territory. Professional
and amateur producers should contact the nearest Samuel French
office or licensing partner to verify availability.

MUSIC USE NOTE

Licensees are solely responsible for obtaining formal written permission from copyright owners to use copyrighted music in the performance of this play and are strongly cautioned to do so. If no such permission is obtained by the licensee, then the licensee must use only original music that the licensee owns and controls. Licensees are solely responsible and liable for all music clearances and shall indemnify the copyright owners of the play(s) and their licensing agent, Samuel French, against any costs, expenses, losses and liabilities arising from the use of music by licensees. Please contact the appropriate music licensing authority in your territory for the rights to any incidental music.

IMPORTANT BILLING AND CREDIT REQUIREMENTS

If you have obtained performance rights to this title, please refer to your licensing agreement for important billing and credit requirements.

CHARACTERS
(*in order of appearance*)

BRONIAN PENDRICK — a theatrical producer
ANNABEL HOLMES — his secretary
RORY MADDEN — his general factotum
ANDREW KIMMER — a neophyte playwright
ALISON BLAIR — a well-known actress
FRIEDA NEBCOTT — a Broadway columnist
CHARLES CARPENTER — an amiable actor
V. NELSON SLOMBER — an undertaker

Locale: New York City
Time: The present

Act One: Bronian's Apartment, early evening, late summer
Act Two: The same, the following morning
Act Three: The same, a few hours later

[NOTE: "Bronian" rhymes with "Smithsonian".]

And Then I Wrote

ACT ONE

The Manhattan apartment of theatrical producer BRONIAN PENDRICK, in the East Seventies, on an evening in late summer. [See "Stage Setting" art.] A few sightline-details you should know about the set: When the four-section accordion-doors to the balcony are fully open, they are out of view of the audience; the cafe-curtains on the dinette window are short, in two rows, and "trim" the window rather than block much of the view through it; the dinette window itself starts about two feet from platform and ends about one foot from ceiling, so there is plenty of sky/skyline to be seen through it; when the balcony-drapes are closed, and the room-lighting dims [during daylight-hours, of course], the dinette area remains bright and cheery, but the rest *of the room goes to about half-normal brightness; during night-scenes, any visible buildings in the sky-line-part of backdrop should show a scattering of lighted windows, and — if possible — a* very *few stars [since Manhattan's lights tend to make star-gazing almost impossible] should be seen in sky-part of backdrop.*

At curtain-rise, the stage is empty of people; there is an untidy stack of mail upon hassock; room lighting is late-summer-evening dark; sky through dinette window and closed balcony doors [these are glass-paneled French doors] is sunset-hued, but this reddish look will fade to full night-darkness within first ten minutes of act.

5

A moment or two after curtain-rise, DOORBELL RINGS. After about five seconds, DOORBELL RINGS AGAIN. Then bedroom door opens, and BRONIAN enters from bedroom. He is in pajamas, and barefoot, and slipping into a bathrobe. When presentable, this man of forty-plus years is not unpleasant of aspect; right now, however, he looks unshaven and rumpled, hair mussed, eyes squinting and blinking blearily. As he lurches toward foyer, he manages to collide with sofa and almost trip over hassock. When he finally gets his sense of direction straight, and is headed directly toward foyer door, DOORBELL RINGS AGAIN. He staggers back a step, heels of hands to temples, as if the sound caused him physical pain, then stumbles forward and flips on lightswitch in foyer; ROOM LIGHTS UP FULL; he unlocks — but does not open — hall door, reels back a pace, changes direction and veers kitchenward as DOORBELL RINGS AGAIN. He shouts doorward, while still lurching doggedly kitchenward:

BRONIAN. It's open, it's open! (*exits into kitchen*)

(*ANNABEL HOLMES enters from hall. She is struggling with an armload of bound scripts, which she sets, with relief, beside mail on hassock. She goes to mirror to check her appearance. It is charming in an end-of-a-wearisome-day fashion. She makes the best of it with a few hair-pats, shoulder-squarings and skirt-tugs, then gives up with a wry shrug, crosses to bedroom and knocks.*)

ANNABEL. Mr. Pendrick? It's Annabel. It's almost half-past seven!

BRONIAN. (*enters from kitchen carrying cup of coffee*) A.M. or P.M.?

ANNABEL. P.M. . . . as in post mortem. (*She gestures toward terrace.*) Why do you think it's getting dark out?

BRONIAN. I thought I might be going blind. (*sips on coffee*)

ANNABEL. Mr. Pendrick, you're not even dressed!

BRONIAN. (*looks down at himself*) That's all right . . . I expect to be dead soon, anyway.

ANNABEL. Everyone will *be* here at eight!

BRONIAN. (*setting cup on pier table*) They'll never get in. There's barely enough room for my temples. (*leans forearm on* DS. *kitchen door jamb, head on forearm*) I'll be back in a minute.

ANNABEL. (*goes to him, takes his other arm*) What time did you get to bed anyhow?

BRONIAN. (*straightens, but keeps forearm over eyes*) It was either two thirty or twelve past six. I couldn't tell which hand was longer.

ANNABEL. (*guiding him toward bedroom*) You'd better take a good cold shower.

BRONIAN. (*arm still over eyes*) Sadist! (*gropes way into bedroom, leaving door open as he exits*)

(*ANNABEL grabs coffee cup and pops briefly into kitchen to get rid of it, then comes down to mound of mail. Through bedroom doorway we hear the SHOWER go on and an instant later an ANGUISHED SHRIEK from BRONIAN. ANNABEL veers, shuts off sound by closing bedroom door, then returns to hassock and lifts heap of mail in both arms. DOORBELL RINGS. ANNABEL wavers, hovers, then drops mail fluttering to floor and answers door. RORY MADDEN enters, in suit but no topcoat, then stops, arms akimbo, surveying mail.*)

RORY. Somebody mug a mailman?

ANNABEL. (*sarcastically*) HA HA HA . . . Rory, as long as you're early you can help me clean up this mess. (*on knees, starts handing him the mail*)

RORY. Where is Friend Bronian? Massaging his bent elbow?

ANNABEL. Our blithe and effervescent host is just going into shock in his shower stall. Will you see he gets back here alive and reasonably presentable?

RORY. (*placing last of mail on hassock*) Okay. If I'm not back in ten minutes, come after both of us. And bring a good-looking friend. (*exits into bedroom, shuts door*)

ANNABEL. (*gets up, sees mail*) This is where I came in! (*Starts to pick it up; DOORBELL RINGS; ANNABEL flings letters wildly into the air, starts for the front door while they're still fluttering down, opens it. ANDREW KIMMER enters in buttoned-up topcoat, smiles with taut uncertainty, then stands looking at her. She indicates mail on floor.*) Please say you're a vacuum cleaner salesman.

ANDREW. I'm looking for Mr. Pendrick.

ANNABEL. So is he. Come on in, whoever you are. (*Shuts door as he enters, then she enters room, kicks a fallen letter out of her way and slumps in left arm chair.*) I'm Annabel Holmes.

ANDREW. (*sees mail, stoops and starts to pick it up*) I'm Andrew Kimmer.

ANNABEL. I thought so. I typed all those nice long letters Mr. Pendrick sent you.

ANDREW. It's all been quite unsettling. I mean exciting.

ANNABEL. Don't give up on that first version yet. Is this—(*indicates pile of scripts*)—your first play?

ANDREW. Is *what* my first play? . . . You mean—those are *it?* It's *them?* (*straightens, drops mail*) It looks just like a real script! (*picks up a script*) And it's got my name on it!

ANNABEL. Well, there are laws.

ANDREW. I can't tell you how exciting this is for me. (*sits in upstage armchair, opens script*) Will you *look* at it! My words, exactly as I wrote them back in Peoria!

ANNABEL. Uh . . . don't get *too* attached to them, Andrew . . . (*BRONIAN enters from bedroom, clad only in shoes, socks and shorts, forearm over eyes and carrying an Alka-Seltzer bottle in his other hand; he is led by RORY, who is carrying a soaped back brush; as they cross up toward kitchen, ANDREW stands, hand extended to shake.*) Mr. Pendrick, this is Andrew Kimmer.

RORY. (*as he and BRONIAN continue onward*) Mr. Kimmer, this is Annabel Holmes.

ANDREW. (*tracking them with unshaken hand*) How do you—(*They exit into kitchen.*)—do? (*drops hand*)

ANNABEL. He'll shake it as soon as he can see it, Andrew. Try to relax.

ANDREW. (*sits back in armchair*) Which one was Mr. Pendrick?

ANNABEL. The one in the Emperor's new clothes.

(*BRONIAN and RORY enter from kitchen, BRONIAN carrying a paper cup filled with fizzing liquid, his eyes now open to a squint; RORY carries both back brush and Alka-Seltzer bottle; they cross bedroomward without pausing, during:*)

BRONIAN. Annabel, remind me to get refills for my paper-cup dispenser.

ANNABEL. Get refills for your paper-cup dispenser.

RORY. We'll be right with you Mr. Kimmer. (*ANDREW stands.*)

BRONIAN. Make yourself at home. (*ANDREW sits. BRONIAN and RORY exit into bedroom, shut door.*)

ANNABEL. Had enough excitement for one night?

ANDREW. What? Oh. I love it! Every minute. It's like the culmination of a dream. Just being here. Don't you?

ANNABEL. (*lost*) Don't I what?

ANDREW. Love just being here in New York, and all?

ANNABEL. (*musing aloud*) I suppose I did when I *first* arrived, but the thrill wore off in a few days.

ANDREW. How long have you been here?

ANNABEL. I was born here.

ANDREW. (*absorbs this; then*) Who did you say that other man was?

ANNABEL. The one with the brush? That's Rory Madden, our general poo-bah!

ANDREW. Is that an official title?

ANNABEL. Rory has too many slots to fit into for a really accurate job-title. He makes sure incoming scripts get read, outgoing scripts get posted, costumes arrive before opening night, hotel bills get paid — All the little odds and ends that have to get done to get the show on. None is enough to keep a full time man busy, so, Rory Madden does *everything*.

ANDREW. Then what does Mr. *Pendrick* do?

ANNABEL. He worries a lot.

ANDREW. Do *you* think "Noblesse Oblige" is a good show?

ANNABEL. I never heard of it.

ANDREW. That's *my* show.

ANNABEL. Oh! Um . . . actually, only Rory and Mr. Pendrick have had a chance to read it, except for Alison

Blair. She's going to let us know what she thinks to-night.

ANDREW. *The* Alison Blair?

ANNABEL. There's another one?

ANDREW. (*stands, wide-eyed*) Alison Blair! Here! Tonight! Right in the same room with me. Giving *her* opinion of *my* script!

ANNABEL. (*trying to curb his rapture a bit*) She's *only* five-foot-four, Andrew.

ANDREW. (*suddenly sits, apprehensive*) Gosh, what if she doesn't *like* it?

ANNABEL. She'll *still* be five-foot-four. (*remembers mess on carpet*) But she won't like the morning mail all over the carpet. (*starts to pick up letters*)

ANDREW. (*not hopefully*) Can I give you a hand?

ANNABEL. No thanks.

ANDREW. (*settles back gratefully*) Thanks. I wonder if the part's *big* enough for her?

ANNABEL. (*still cleaning up the mess*) What's your play *about,* Andrew?

ANDREW. Well, "Noblesse Oblige" is a French expression. It means that people in important positions have corresponding obligations.

ANNABEL. (*rising with letters*) Andrew—Promise me I'll be the last person you'll ever tell that.

ANDREW. (*embarrassed*) I wasn't trying to show off.

ANNABEL. Some people might not realize that. What's the *plot* about?

(*During the next speech, ANNABEL stashes mail on bar, returns to left armchair. She listens to AN-DREW politely at first, then with incredulity, and by the end of his eager resumé, she is goggle-eyed with disbelief, in a dazed, dumbfounded trance.*

ANDREW remains oblivious to ANNABEL's reaction to his spiel, throughout.)

ANDREW. (*a self-enthralling author*) Well, it starts on a cotton plantation — in the South. There's this big family, The Calhouns, ruled by the grandmother, Letitia Calhoun. She's very hard on them, because they're all weaklings, but she likes them. Of course she doesn't let them know it. Well, one day her son Ralph gets the chance to sell the cotton crop to a northern blanket manufactureer, Harold Stebbins. Harold is really just interested in Ralph's daughter Olivia, and is using blanket manufacturing as a cover-up. Well, Letitia finds out, and tries to tell Ralph the mistake he's making. She figures that once the marriage takes place, Harold will call off the deal, and by then their regular cotton-buyers will be shopping elsewhere. Meanwhile, the daughter falls in love with Frank Jericho, the grocer in the town, who has secretly loved her for years, and has been helping the family survive by giving them free groceries. Frank, by the way, is the youngest son of Bill Jericho, the only man Letitia ever really loved, but her proud family wouldn't let her marry Bill because he was only a grocer, just like Frank. In memory of his father, at first, and then later because he loves Olivia, Frank has been helping the Calhouns survive. All they really have left is their social position. The servants all know the family's poor, but they stay on, anyhow, because they're all too loyal to work someplace else. Well, Olivia finds out there's no money, and she decides she'll have to go through with the marriage to the blanket manufacturer so the Calhouns will be rich again. But Frank the grocer thinks Olivia *loves* Harold, and — on the night Harold is coming to dinner — Frank refuses to send any free groceries. So Ralph, the father, goes into town to plead with Frank to let them have one last night's credit, because once he sells the cotton to Harold, he'll be able to pay off the grocery, bank loan, utilities, and everything. This makes Frank even madder, to think that Ralph thinks he kept them in groceries just to have a lot of income coming, so he pretends to go along with Ralph, and sends the groceries same as usual, except that he puts poison in the wine, so that when Harold toasts the bride-to-be, he'll die. Then, just as he's closing up the shop, one of the servants stops by with a message thanking him, from the daughter Olivia, who sends her love. In this same conversation, it comes out that Harold is a teetotaler, so it will be the grandmother who proposes the toast. So Harold starts racing for the house to stop her. But just as he bursts into the dining room, the grandmother has just finished the toast, and she falls dead. Frank confesses his crime, and is attacked by Harold, the blanket-manufacturer, from the north. Harold tries to make Frank drink the poisoned wine, and the sight of this is too much for Olivia, who loves Frank, and she goes out of her mind, talking to the grandmother's empty chair as if Letitia were still alive. Now Ralph, her father, realizes it's all his fault, because of his greed about the cotton, and he orders Harold out of his house. The sheriff comes for poor Frank the grocer, and the daughter is taken off to a madhouse, and Ralph falls on his knees beside the body of his dead mother and sobs for forgiveness, and we hear an unseen chorus singing *Swanee River* as the lights dim and the curtain slowly falls!

ANNABEL. *Wow, what a plot!*

ANDREW. You wanna hear what happens in Act *Two*—?

(*As ANNABEL reacts, the DOORBELL RINGS.*)

ANNABEL. Hold it, Tennessee! I want another witness. (*Answers door; ALISON BLAIR enters; she is only five-foot-four, just as postulated, but every inch an actress.*) Hello, Alison! Your watch must be fast. You're right on time.

ALISON. I couldn't wait to see Bronian another minute! . . . About this marvelous play! . . . All right, I couldn't wait to see Bronian.

ANNABEL. I didn't say a word.

ALISON. Your reticence was eloquent. (*She sees bound scripts; picks one up, sits in left armchair with it.*) Ah, yes, this is much better. The carbon Bronian sent me was a bit smudged in places.

ANDREW. I erase a lot.

ANNABEL. Andrew Kimmer, our talented author.

ANDREW. I'm not really.

ALISON. Then who the hell *are* you?

ANNABEL. He means not talented.

ALISON. You have no right to be modest about this play, Andrew. Don't you agree Annabel?

ANNABEL. So far, it's a regular "Gone With The Windy Little Foxes Into Another Part Of The Forest With A Cat On A Hot Tin Jezebel From Beulah Land!" . . . I can't speak for acts two and three.

ALISON. Wait till you *read* them. There's a maternity scene at the end of the second act that makes "Room Service" look like something out of Ibsen! (*ANDREW reacts with shock.*)

ANNABEL. You mean Olivia gets married after all?

ALISON. That's what's so hilarious. She can't *remember!* Her father is simply furious, of course. The family honor is at stake, but he doesn't know who to shoot!

ANNABEL. If she *is* married, why doesn't the *father* of the child admit it?

ALISON. He promised Olivia *she* could break the news to her family in her own way, but it's taken her nine months to build up her courage.

ANNABEL. And now she needs it all to face the delivery room?

ALISON. Not *quite* all: She *does* manage—just as her labor pains start—to run up to her father and shout, "Guess what!?" (*Both women shriek with laughter, then see ANDREW's face and sober slightly.*)

ANNABEL. Andrew—Is there anything wrong?

ANDREW. "Noblesse Oblige" isn't a comedy! . . . It's a deeply meaningful drama. Sorrow, pain, misery, raw emotion and endless pathos!

ALISON. (*to ANNABEL*) Does Bronian know that?

ANNABEL. I doubt it!

ANDREW. What do you mean?

ALISON. Darling, try to understand . . . Bronian Pendrick feels—Well. . . ? (*looks to ANNABEL for help*)

ANNABEL. He figures the average person's life is tough enough without spending two hours watching even *worse* troubles. His approach to theatre is—Well—? (*looks to ALISON for help*)

ALISON. There's enough rain falling into people's lives without him poking holes in their umbrellas.

ANNABEL. So Mister Pendrick provides a cozy comfort station between the eight-thirty curtain and the eleven o'clock news.

ANDREW. But, there are more important things in life than having a good time! You can't expect an audience to deny *that*?

ALISON. Nobody wants to *deny* it. They just want to *forget* it!

ANDREW. Isn't there any hope for a *serious* dramatist?!

ALISON. Of course! There are *plenty* of people around who feel their life isn't tough *enough* without a theatrical *assist!*

ANNABEL. And look on the *practical* side, Andrew—

ANDREW. What do you mean?

ALISON. Do you have *any* idea how *tough* it is to get a producer interested in doing the play of an *unknown* writer?

ANDREW. Well, certainly, but—!

ANNABEL. Take a friendly tip. Let Bronian do the show in his own way and make you a name. *Then* you can concentrate on making people miserable!

ALISON. The important thing, right now, is to get your play *done!*

ANDREW. But I want it done *properly.* I want it done *just* the way I first envisioned it. *Every* playwright does.

ANNABEL. But why should *you* be the first?

ALISON. And that *plot* of yours has such great comic *potential*—!

ANDREW. (*nearly in tears*) Look . . . I'll admit there may be a *slight* touch of the ludicrous in my show, but that's not actual *comedy.* It's what you call "humor of recognition." People always laugh at their own foibles when they see them on the stage. It can't be helped.

ALISON. (*dryly*) But it's been so *long* since I poisoned anybody's grandmother . . .

ANDREW. (*exasperation blows his misery away*) Not *specific* foibles! Just—*life* as it is *really lived!*

ALISON. (*to ANNABEL*) Remind me not to propose any toasts!

ANDREW. Miss Blair—be logical—how could you *play* the part as anything *but* tragic?

ALISON. (*shrugs*) I can *always* twine magnolia blossoms in my braids.

ANDREW. (*bemused*) Somehow I didn't *envision* the grandmother in braids.

ALISON. (*stiffens, sits up tall and wrathful*) *Who* said anything about the damn *grandmother?!*

ANNABEL. (*quickly*) Uh, Andrew—*Alison* is up for the role of *Olivia.*

ANDREW. (*without thinking; to ANNABEL:*) The *daughter?!* But—*she's* only seventeen years *old!* (*abruptly realizing he's on thin ice, he continues, after a pause, to ALISON:*) —uh—*aren't* you?

ALISON. (*holds pose, then relaxes and laughs, observing to ANNABEL:*) That's *pretty* neat choreography for a guy with *both feet* in his mouth!

(*BRONIAN enters from bedroom, now dapper, combed and shaven; he hurries immediately to ALISON.*)

BRONIAN. Alison-Baby!

ALISON. Bronian, my dear! (*They embrace, briefly, as RORY enters from bedroom, extends arms toward ANNABEL.*)

RORY. Sweetheart, it's been ages!

ANNABEL. Lets not over-excite Mr. Kimmer.

BRONIAN. (*breaks clinch, goes to ANDREW*) So you're Andrew Kimmer! I want to tell you I am honored to make your acquaintance. The moment I began reading your play I knew I was in cahoots with greatness. What keen insights! What a remarkable grasp of conflict, pathos, tragedy! (*ANNABEL and ALISON exchange a bewildered look with each other, then with ANDREW, who looks just as bewildered but definitely relieved.*) "Noblesse Oblige" is brilliant! A masterpiece

of inspired imagination and thrilling emotional cathar-
sis!

ANNABEL. (*dryly*) And wait'll you read Act *Two!*

BRONIAN. (*annoyed*) Of course, it needs a bit of fixing, but that's why we're all *here* tonight!

ALISON. I was *wondering* about that . . .

RORY. Andrew, when *we* are through cutting and
polishing your rough diamond it will sparkle like—
Wondering about *what?*

ALISON. Why we're meeting *here* at *night,* instead of
Bronian's *office* during the *day!*

BRONIAN. (*quickly*) Now, uh, *Alison*—!

ANDREW. Oh, *I* don't mind meeting at night. Though
I *did* think *you'd* be at *work,* being an *actress.*

ALISON. Don't rub it in. But Bronian—Why *are* we
meeting at night?

BRONIAN. (*quickly but lamely*) I couldn't *wait* till
morning to talk to Andrew!

ANNABEL. (*to ANDREW*) If he's caught by the sun-
rise he turns to dust.

BRONIAN. (*irked*) Annabel, do something useful.

ANNABEL. (*shrugs, complies*) Here, Andrew, let me
take your coat!

ANDREW. Thanks.

(*During next speech, he removes it, and stands revealed
in a hot pink turtleneck shirt and a large-check
tangerine-and-turquoise sportcoat.*)

BRONIAN. Yours is a drama of such power, such impact, such deep meaning, such . . . (*sees outfit and
reacts*) . . . such an ensemble!

ANDREW. I ransacked *Peoria* to find it!

ALISON. Ye gods, *why?!*

ANDREW. I wanted to look like someone in *theatre*.

ANNABEL. (*aside, to RORY*) Theatre of the *absurd?*

BRONIAN. (*recovering*) Let's get down to business! Everybody grab a script and we'll begin our analysis!

(*Seating: BRONIAN to left armchair, ALISON to upstage armchair, with ANNABEL, RORY and ANDREW on sofa.*)

ALISON. Excuse me, but — *What* are we going to *analyze?*

BRONIAN. Structure related to character. The *motivations* bother me.

ALISON. The motivations are perfectly *clear!*

BRONIAN. That's what *bothers* me! In today's theatre, the more mystifying the spectators' experience, the bigger your chance for a hit.

ALISON. Bronian, the *last* mystifying drama that opened in this town had the theatre critics chorusing, "What's it all about, Albee?"!

BRONIAN. Bah, what do *critics* know?!

ALISON. A hundred easy ways to close a play.

BRONIAN. But damn it, this play *needs* symbolism, mysterious events, odd characters, strange references which are never explained — ! (*to ANDREW*) Can't I even *suggest* a few of them to you?

ANDREW. (*warily*) Such as — ?

BRONIAN. (*waxing enthusiastic*) Well, for instance — Letitia always goes around with an ivory-headed cane. *Why?*

ANDREW. (*shrugs*) She's got a bad back!

BRONIAN. You call that *motivation?!*

ANDREW. (*flustered*) Well—uh—*also,* the cane's her badge of *authority* . . . she *waves* it a lot during arguments.

BRONIAN. (*conspiratorily*) Ah, but *what if,* instead of walking with a cane, she always rides a *pogo stick?!*

RORY. (*enthused*) Hey, I *like* that!

ANDREW. (*going out of his mind*) *What* would an *old lady* be doing on a *pogo stick?!*

ALISON. Hanging on for dear life.

ANNABEL. And screaming a lot.

BRONIAN. *If* she actually *is* an old lady, sure! But . . . *is* she?

ANDREW. (*almost in tears*) The woman is a *grandmother!*

ANNABEL. Well, wait—Elizabeth Taylor's a grandmother, and you wouldn't call *her* an old lady . . .

ALISON. (*dryly*) If you valued your life.

ANDREW. I'm going to be sick.

BRONIAN. Wait till I finish my analysis!

ALISON. —and you'll be even sicker!

RORY. Bronian, what did you mean—*Is* she an old lady?

BRONIAN. What if she's a figment of the grocer's tortured imagination, a symbol of his guilt materialized from his own mind to plague him?

ALISON. How guilty can a man feel about poisoning his own figment?!

BRONIAN. Don't bother me with details. That's Andrew's problem. Annabel—aren't you taking notes?

ANNABEL. You said *everyone* grab a script. Who's got a pencil?

RORY. Here.

BRONIAN. (*as ANNABEL takes pencil from RORY*) By the way Alison, what do you think of Charles Carpenter as your leading man?

ALISON. (*incredulous*) What *can* I think of a man who calls his dalmatian "Spot"?

RORY. He *is* kind of an *oddball*, Bronian . . .

BRONIAN. Never mind. A director can *always* rely on a trained actor's *professional* instincts.

ALISON. But we were talking about Charles Carpenter!

ANNABEL. The last time a director trusted Charles' instincts he played Willie Loman like Benny Hill on vacation.

ALISON. Say, who *is* directing, come to think of it?

RORY. (*with shy pride*) *I* am.

ANNABEL. (*stunned*) Rory, *you've* never directed a play in your *life!*

BRONIAN. Nevertheless, Rory proved the best man of all the competition.

ANNABEL. Who did he beat out?

ALISON. Probably Charles Carpenter.

ANDREW. Could I have a brandy? My mouth is going dry.

ANNABEL. (*heading for bar*) I'll make it a double. Anybody else want anything?

ALISON. I hope somebody has a spare cigarette. I'm fresh out.

BRONIAN. (*patting his pockets*) So am I. Rory—run down to the delicatessen and get some. Oh, and get the evening paper. I want to see Frieda Nebcott's column.

RORY. (*en route to door*) You left her in shape to write it? (*exits*)

ANNABEL. So *that's* where you were till all hours of the morning.

BRONIAN. A producer has to stay in the columnists' good graces.

ALISON. Frieda Nebcott has the good graces of a pain-crazed tarantula.

ANDREW. (*surprised*) Just last week she wished you a happy birthday in her column. . . ?

ALISON. Did she have to mention *which* birthday?

BRONIAN. Now Alison, you're *not* exactly ready for *Medicare!*

ALISON. But I'm feeling *readier* every *day!*

ANDREW. How old *are* you? . . . I mean, how *young?* . . . I mean —

ANNABEL. Shall we get back to the *other* little old lady?

ALISON. (*with good-natured chagrin*) Thanks a *lot!*

BRONIAN. Where did we leave off?

ANNABEL. (*checks notes*) We just put Letitia on a pogo stick.

ANDREW. Look . . . I don't like to be a killjoy, but — *I'm* not fussy about a *line* here and there, or a slight shifting of sequence, you understand — but you're uprooting the entire *concept* of the role!

BRONIAN. (*flinging arms out in despair*) This is the thanks I get! I find a play, quite a good play, by an absolute unknown . . . I send him plane tickets to get him here to New York . . . I offer him a production, with big name stars . . . and then he stubbornly refuses to have experienced people in the profession make a few *simple* little suggestions — !

ANDREW. "Simple"? Figments on pogo sticks?!

BRONIAN. (*slumps back into chair*) Can somebody explain to this man what we are trying to accomplish?

ALISON. Love to . . . (*pause*) What *are* we trying to accomplish?

BRONIAN. Alison, if you had any grasp of today's theatre, you'd know! It's not *enough* to have a well-written play any more. A show must also be something the audience *wants!*

ALISON. Maybe I'm simpleminded, but I always thought they just wanted a *good show!*

BRONIAN. *Listen* . . . Between TV, movies, theatre, books and so on, there just isn't anything *new.* An author needs a *gimmick* to keep the audience interested. I'm *not* trying to do the entire play *over,* I just want to prop up the *sags!*

ANNABEL. Well, maybe if you just explained your ideas in *theory,* Andrew could do the rewrites in his *own* way, Bronian.

ANDREW. (*with a faint flutter of hope*) That *would* be a *big* help. Some of your *specific* suggestions have been a bit startling . . .

BRONIAN. But Andrew, the author with knowhow today *fills* his play with mystery and shock value. The more bizarre the better.

ANDREW. But an *imaginary* grandmother. . . ?! While we're at it why not make the daughter a Chinese laundress?!

(*ANDREW sees their overjoyed reaction to his absurd suggestion; during the following he looks lost and helplessly from one to the other.*)

BRONIAN. *Great!* Annabel—?

ANNABEL. (*scribbling furiously*) Got it!

BRONIAN. Terrific!

ALISON. Oh no! Not *my* role? Please? *I* can't play a *laundress!*

ANNABEL. Why not?

ALISON. My doctor told me to avoid *starches!* (*When OTHERS all glare at her joke, she pats at her tresses as she self-teases:*) Luckily, he said *nothing* about *bleach!*

BRONIAN. (*snaps fingers*) Bleach! What an idea!

Listen—She gets high on the fumes . . . and that's when . . .

ANDREW. (*almost sobbing*) No oh no oh no oh no oh no . . .

RORY. (*enters with newspaper and cigarettes*) Here you are. How's it going?

BRONIAN. (*business of opening pack, offering one to ALISON, lighting both, etc*) We'll test it out on you. What do you think about the daughter being a Chinese laundress?

ANDREW. (*slightly tipsy*) Does anybody want to know what *I* think?

ANNABEL. What *do* you think?

ANDREW. (*as others focus on him, waiting*) . . . I think I'll have another brandy.

RORY. (*to BRONIAN, handing him newspaper*) What did that Nebcott dame *promise* you, anyhow?

BRONIAN. (*looking through paper*) *I* did all the promising, Rory.

ALISON. (*reacts with more than casual interest*) Really? And what's *she* doing? Reminiscing in print?

RORY. For a dinner date that broke up at six A.M., her plug isn't very *long!*

BRONIAN. How do *you* know what time our dinner date broke up?

RORY. *That's* what time you fell over the *hassock* . . . and Frieda wasn't *with* you.

ALISON. (*sighs*) What a pity.

ANNABEL. (*to ANDREW, coming back with a full glass*) Careful. In large doses that stuff can be fatal.

ANDREW. Promise?

BRONIAN. What were you *doing* here at six A.M. this morning?

RORY. Keeping our appointment for ten P.M. last *night.*

BRONIAN. Rory! I'm sorry! I completely forgot! You should have gone home.

RORY. I probably would have, but I must've dozed off in the chair around eleven o'clock. Anyhow, no harm done. You'd never have gotten undressed without help.

BRONIAN. You put me to bed? I don't remember a thing.

RORY. I'll fill you in. I woke up at the sound of the crash, picked you up, got you into pajamas and bed, went downstairs and found your car illegally parked, the keys still in it and the headlights on, put it in a space three blocks away, came back to return your keys, found your milk and the morning mail and brought it in, left the keys on your dresser and staggered home myself.

BRONIAN. Strange. I *seem* to remember reading the *mail*. But—if Rory put me to bed at six—when did I get up again?

ANNABEL. Never mind that. What does La Nebcott have to say?

BRONIAN. (*finding item*) Ah! "On the Broadway scene, talented producer Bronian Pendrick confides to me—"

ALISON. How do you confide to a public address system?

BRONIAN. "—that he has a hot new property which is going to make the critics in this town sit up and take notice . . ."

ANDREW. (*muzzily*) "*Give* notice" is more like it! . . . Chinese pogo sticks. . . !

BRONIAN. Andrew, come up out of that well of self-pity and listen to this: "The author, a fresh new talent from Peoria, may be the very shot in the arm a drooping New York Stage needs." (*pauses*)

RORY. (*enthused*) Go *on*. . . !

BRONIAN. (*a little miffed*) That's *it!*

ALISON. It took you till *six* this morning to wangle *two* lousy lines? (*She stands as she says this and ANDREW — woozy & grateful — slips behind her and sinks leadenly into chair.*)

BRONIAN. Not to mention seventy-four dollars in cash and fifteen kilowatts of charm to get that item planted where my backers would see it.

ANDREW. (*awakened from his torpor*) I didn't know the New York stage was drooping.

ANNABEL. Frieda Nebcott just likes to go around scaring people with her column five days a week.

ANDREW. Why?

ALISON. It beats once a year on a broomstick.

ANDREW. Mr. Pendrick, why didn't she mention me or the play by name?

ALISON. He ran out of kilowatts.

BRONIAN. Listen, I'll be honest: I *asked* her not to. Play-production is a risky business. If Andrew had decided not to sign with me tonight, I'd have peddled somebody else's play to my backers. They'd never know the difference.

ALISON. Of course, the author would have to move to Peoria.

BRONIAN. I had to give her *some* kind of detail. Anyhow, this is all beside the point now that Andrew *has* signed.

ANDREW. But I haven't.

BRONIAN. Annabel! That was the very first thing you were supposed to attend to when he showed up.

ANNABEL. I was distracted by the Alka-Seltzer parade. And have you forgotten the very first thing *you* were supposed to attend to was to *give* me the contracts when I showed up?

ALISON. You mean after seventy-four bucks and fifteen kilowatts, Andrew is still walking around free?

ANDREW. Free to do what? How many other places could I peddle my play before my plane leaves in the morning?

BRONIAN. *Tomorrow* morning? What do you think I flew you in here for . . . an autograph?

ANDREW. I thought I was here to meet you and sign the contract. I have to be back at work tomorrow afternoon. I promised my boss.

BRONIAN. How do you expect to work on a script in Peoria?

ALISON. He did all right on the *first* draft, Bronian.

BRONIAN. *As* a first draft, *yes!* But that script still needs *tons* of rewrites, and my *author* is flying *home* in the morning!

ANNABEL. I wrote Andrew *exactly* what you dictated!

ANDREW. There wasn't a *word* about my staying on! How did *I* know the script wasn't perfect? I mean, *why* would a producer offer a *contract* for a script he didn't *like?!*

BRONIAN. You idiot, that's *show business!* Producers *never* get perfect scripts—they *expect* rewrites—a contract is just my way of placing a bet on the author's instincts for self-preservation!

ANDREW. I sure couldn't handle my *Peoria* job on that instinct.

ALISON. What line of work *doesn't* rely on self-preservation?

ANDREW. I'm an apprentice mortician.

ALISON. (*instantly snaps fingers, looks delightedly toward ANNABEL*) I *just* figured out his "humor of recognition"!

BRONIAN. Annabel, *where* are those *contracts?!*

ANNABEL. (*who has been going through the mail*) The contracts aren't here, just the empty envelope. Should I phone your lawyer?

BRONIAN. If he mailed me an empty envelope, he's *not* my lawyer!

ALISON. Bronian, are you sure you didn't put them someplace yourself?

BRONIAN. I wouldn't put it past me! But — Where? What the hell would I do with them?

ANDREW. Remember, I haven't said *yes* —

BRONIAN. You will!

ALISON. (*semi-vamps close to ANDREW*) We have *ways* of making people sign . . .

ANNABEL. We call them royalties.

ALISON. (*cheek-to-cheek with ANDREW, on the arm of his chair*) You'll sign, Andrew . . . For Alison? . . . Won't you? (*coaxing*) Pretty please?

BRONIAN. Conserve your kilowatts. We haven't even got the damn *contracts* yet! That dream . . . if I could only remember . . . There was a dragon . . .

ALISON. Well, we're back to Frieda again!

BRONIAN. Quiet! (*eyes shut, fists at temples:*) The dragon . . . was after me. I — I had the contracts in my fist, rolled up . . . like a sword. That's it! The dragon was dusty and shabby, and — somehow — I knew it represented approaching poverty! But the contracts represented potential profit . . . So I held them in my fist, and — and — I —

ANDREW. (*to ALISON, at this pregnant pause*) Are you sure we're here to analyze the *play?*

ANNABEL. (*calming BRONIAN*) Let's be logical. They must be someplace in the apartment.

RORY. A search! Come on, everybody just pick a room and *SEARCH!*

ANNABEL. I'll take the terrace—

RORY. I'll investigate the kitchen—

BRONIAN. Andrew, you check the bedroom and bath.

ALISON. (*when ANDREW hesitates*) Be a sport! We want your name on a contract, not your head on a platter.

ANNABEL. You shouldn't have told him. We could've appealed to his humor of recognition. (*exits to terrace*)

ANDREW. Oh . . . All right, all right!

(*RORY and ANDREW make their respective exits on:*)

ALISON. Bronian and I will search in here . . . (*sees OTHERS are out of earshot; then:*) Bronian . . . What's going on?

BRONIAN. (*very uneasily*) What do you mean?

ALISON. You know very well what I mean, Bronian Pendrick!

BRONIAN. I do?

ALISON. Yes . . . you do. Rory directing the show. . . ?! Really! And meeting here instead of at your office. *And* this insanity about a "deeply meaningful drama". Hmmm? Oh . . . and when I tried phoning you this morning your service didn't answer. (*pause*) Bronian—are you broke?

BRONIAN. (*with a deep sigh*) Yes, damn it! And that witch Frieda Nebcott knows it. You don't think I'd date that woman of my own volition?

ALISON. (*changing the subject*) Tell me—honestly now—what you think of Andrew's play. Not how good it is, but *what* it is.

BRONIAN. What do you *think* it is?

ALISON. I think your high-sounding praises of its dramatic merit are mere catering to Nebcott's constant complaint about the theatre's lack of meaningful offerings. What are you up to?

BRONIAN. I promise I'll tell you, but I can't talk now in front of the others. Trust me . . . please?

ALISON. I think I do trust you, but what did you tell Frieda Nebcott?

BRONIAN. I told her that if my backers didn't find out how desperately I need them—I'd . . . well . . . I said I'd make it worth her while.

ALISON. Oh yeah? How? She's not interested in *money.*

BRONIAN. Everybody's interested in money.

ALISON. If her column could be bought for cash it would be a permanent fixture on every production budget . . . probably the first item! However . . . perhaps she *is* interested in "a certain talented producer" . . .

BRONIAN. Don't be ridiculous . . .

ALISON. (*interrupting him*) Hey! This is me! Remember? You taught me this business from the ground up when you gave me my first role. I know money isn't the only legal tender on Broadway, so don't try to. . . . (*She is interrupted by ANNABEL.*)

ANNABEL. Nothing out there but patio furniture and polluted air.

BRONIAN. Why don't you go give Andrew a hand?

ALISON. He's probably knotting bedsheets together and plotting an escape.

(*ANNABEL leaves and just as she exits, RORY enters.*)

BRONIAN. Rory? Anything?

RORY. Refrigerator, pantry and silverware drawers— no dice. *And* your cupboards make mother Hubbard look like a hoarder.

(*ANDREW re-enters from bedroom.*)

ALISON. Well?

ANDREW. Miss Holmes came in so I thought I should come out.

RORY. They do these things so well in Peoria.

BRONIAN. Get back in there! SEARCH! (*ANDREW goes back into bedroom.*) I've got to think . . . If I had the contracts right now . . . *where* would I hide them?

ALISON. If you had the contracts right now, *why* would you hide them?

BRONIAN. If I *wanted* to . . .

ALISON. A wall safe?

RORY. He hasn't got a wall safe.

ALISON. Well, that solves my Christmas shopping problem.

BRONIAN. CHRISTMAS! . . . Something about—Santa Claus—Why does *Santa Claus* ring a bell?

ALISON. So you can find that brass pot in a blizzard.

RORY. Hold it Alison—I think he's remembering . . .

BRONIAN. Quick . . . Start naming Santa Claus things. . . !

ALISON. (*looking hard at BRONIAN*) A big red nose?

BRONIAN. Har-de-har-har.

(*This next sequence should be done in rapid fire like a word-association test.*)

ALISON. Elves.

RORY. Toys.

ALISON. Milk and cookies.

RORY. Reindeer.

ALISON. North Pole.

RORY. Snow-covered rooftops.

ALISON. White Beard.
RORY. Sleigh bells.
ALISON. Three Wise Men!
RORY. "My Two Front Teeth!"
ALISON. (*sings*) ". . . and a partridge in a pear tree!"
BOTH MEN. (*give ALISON a disdainful look*) Alison!
ALISON. Sorry.
RORY. (*to BRONIAN again*) Fireplaces?
ALISON. Fire! You dreamed about a *dragon?!*
BRONIAN. There's a fireplace in my bedroom—!

(*ALL start for bedroom. They stop as ANNABEL comes out brandishing rolled-up contracts.*)

ANNABEL. Ta-dah!
ALISON. Right from the dragon's mouth.

(*ANNABEL is rather sooty and disheveled-looking.*)

ANNABEL. They were jammed in the flue. I nearly got wedged in the damper trying to retrieve them.
ALISON. Well. . . . Mary Poppins you ain't!
BRONIAN. Where's Andrew?
ANNABEL. Under the bed.
RORY. Doesn't he know that's the first place we'd look for him? (*He exits to bedroom to fetch ANDREW.*)
ANNABEL. I don't think he was hiding . . . just seeking.
BRONIAN. (*takes contracts, wipes off soot and unrolls them, etc.*) Alison, look in the kitchen drawers and see if you can find a pen.
ANNABEL. Excuse me while I clean up a bit.

(*Exits into bedroom as ALISON exits to kitchen;*

BRONIAN lays contracts on coffee table and RORY and ANDREW enter from bedroom.)

ANDREW. Before I sign anything I'd like to talk this over . . .

RORY. Come on Andrew, sign. You can always claim you weren't in your right mind when you did it.

ANDREW. But could I prove it?

BRONIAN. No one who signs a Broadway contract is in his right mind.

ALISON. (*entering from kitchen*) No pen no where! How about a swizzle stick dipped in Jack Daniels?

ANDREW. *Wait,* I've got a pen.

RORY. Alison was only joking. (*takes ANDREW's pen*) This is green ink. Is that legal?

(*ANNABEL re-enters, having cleaned up.*)

BRONIAN. On a contract, intentions are everything. Sign it in green.

ANNABEL. Andrew, about your plane tomorrow—

BRONIAN. Stop reminding him!

ANNABEL. I just want to know which flight he's booked on so I can cancel his reservation for him.

ANDREW. I'm not sure I want it canceled. What about my boss?

BRONIAN. Phone. Say you've got the flu. Your boss will believe you.

ALISON. How do you know?

BRONIAN. Morticians *love* believing people have the flu.

ANDREW. Well, if you feel it's absolutely necessary . . .

ALISON. Oh we do! We do! And once we start staging it so will you. You may want more changes than *we* will.

ANNABEL. And you should be with Rory at all times to make sure it *feels* the way it should.

ALISON. A man who's never directed a play can always use an extra mind.

RORY. What makes you think I want an extra mind?

ANNABEL. With Charles Carpenter in the cast, you'll need it to break even. Charles is the kind of person who visits the dentist to have wisdom teeth put *in*.

ALISON. For all his shortcomings, I must admit he's very co-operative.

ANNABEL. Charles isn't co-operative, he's just too scared to argue. I heard that one of his ancestors was a real live chicken.

BRONIAN. The Carpenters are descended from William the Conqueror. There's not a cowardly bone in his body.

ANNABEL. Then it's just coincidence that his family crest is a doormat licking a boot?

BRONIAN. Charles will be just fine. The critics were very pleased with his last show.

ALISON. Only because they hoped it *was* his last show.

RORY. Walter Kerr, who gave it the *best* review, wrote "It was a very pleasant evening. I laughed at witty dialogue from very talented and charming people. Then the curtain went up . . ."

ANNABEL. Never mind. . . . Please sign, Andrew. Mr. Pendrick won't let you down.

ANDREW. (*hesitating*) Will you leave all the actual alterations to me?

BRONIAN. If you'll promise to keep an open mind. I do think that your colleagues in this enterprise are entitled to make a *few* suggestions.

ANDREW. What *kind* of suggestions?

BRONIAN. *Little* things.

RORY. Tiny, almost unnoticeable things.

ALISON. Just a dab of the polishing cloth here—

ANNABEL. —a spot of paint there—

RORY. Not really changing anything, just . . . heightening certain spots.

BRONIAN. Injecting the characters with an extra spark of life.

ALISON. Take Letitia. She's realistic, in a folksy way, but . . .

RORY. She comes off kind of bland.

ALISON. She needs a few extra idiosyncrasies, Andrew.

BRONIAN. Things that etch her in the audience's mind.

RORY. Right now, she's loveable. With our help she'd be unforgettable.

ANNABEL. No one's saying she's not realistic.

ALISON. She simply needs something to make her different.

ANDREW. She's already got a Chinese granddaughter!!!

BRONIAN. Don't worry your head about details. Just sign the contract.

ANNABEL. All four copies, please.

ANDREW. I do wish I were sure you people know what you're talking about.

ALISON. Welllll . . . that's part of the excitement.

BRONIAN. We're offering you our years of experience.

RORY. Our unswerving loyalty as companions in a common cause.

ANNABEL. Trust us.

BRONIAN. Sign the nice contract. . . ? (*ANDREW almost signs, hesitates.*) I'll make you a deal! (*ANDREW and others look up with interest.*) If you promise to follow my guidelines — on audience appeal, not specific alterations — I promise you I will insist on only one change, verbatim. The title! (*All look at ANDREW hopefully.*)

ANDREW. Only the title? And any other alterations are up to me?

BRONIAN. You have my solemn word in front of three witnesses.

ANDREW. (*steels himself, then signs all four copies with great care*) There!

(*OTHERS go limp with relief; BRONIAN takes pen, signs one copy, hands it to ANDREW.*)

BRONIAN. That's your copy Andrew. (*shakes his hand*) We're in business. This calls for a celebration. Let's everybody have a drink! (*All head for highboy bar.*)

ANNABEL. Now, the first thing to do, Andrew, is to cancel that airplane reservation. Do you have a place to stay?

ANDREW. Not yet. I thought it'd be easy to get a single for one night.

RORY. What about luggage?

ANDREW. Just shaving things and a toothbrush in my topcoat pocket.

BRONIAN. I'll lend you a typewriter.

RORY. I can lend you some clothes.

ALISON. Is there anything else you need?

ANDREW. Well, it's been a while since dinner.

BRONIAN. Rory, make the man a sandwich!

RORY. (*with hocus-pocus gesture*) Poof! You're a sandwich!

(*No one laughs. ANNABEL sighs in RORY's direction
and heads toward phone, which she will bring down
to coffee table.*)

ANNABEL. I'll start calling hotels.

ANDREW. While you're at it would you put a call
through to my boss? It's the V. Nelson Slomber Funeral
Home—

RORY. Come on, Andrew, before you become your
boss's next customer.

(*RORY and ANDREW exit to kitchen; ANNABEL
sits on sofa and starts making calls but cannot be
heard.*)

ALISON. (*at bar with BRONIAN*) You're just *full* of
promises these days. You really intend to change only
the *title?*

BRONIAN. Don't worry. I have a plan.

ALISON. I hope it includes building up the female lead.

BRONIAN. Which part is the female lead?

ALISON. That depends on the buildup. The daughter
has youth, good looks, and a great mad-scene, but
Letitia gets to drink the poisoned wine and die. Luckily,
she remains throughout the next two acts as a visualiza-
tion of the mad daughter's deluded imaginings.

BRONIAN. No other female roles?

ALISON. Well, the cook has a four-line walk-on, waving a soup ladle. And there's a maid who gets to answer
the door. Do you see me as either of those? And watch
how you answer that!

BRONIAN. You know, seriously, there *is* a problem.
You're hardly the grandmother type, but—you must admit—you're not a teen-aged southern belle either.

ALISON. Too bad Olivia hasn't got a *mother*. That'd be just about perfect.

BRONIAN. There's always the *father*. Can you grow sideburns?

ANNABEL. (*hangs up phone and trudges up to them on:*) I've tried three hotels, big ones, and they're all booked solid. There's some convention in town . . . dentists or adventists or something like that. . . .

ALISON. We could get Andrew a white jacket with a Bible in the pocket and let him take his chances.

ANNABEL. I placed the call to Peoria, but the line's busy. The operator's going to try again and ring me back. (*sets phone back on bar*)

BRONIAN. Better try a few more hotels.

ANNABEL. I can't remember any more numbers. Where's your directory?

BRONIAN. By the extension in the bedroom. Keep trying. (*ANNABEL exits into bedroom.*)

ALISON. I don't know why we're even *discussing* the female lead if all you're going to change is the *title*.

BRONIAN. Believe me, that title change will take care of *everything,* including the *sex* problem!

ALISON. There's hardly any sex *in* the script. Or is that the *problem?*

BRONIAN. It won't be when *I* finish with Andrew. *What* kind of realism leaves out sex problems? Everybody's got problems with sex. (*pause*) . . . and *bigotry!* We've *got* to get bigotry into the plot. Bigotry is big this season!

ALISON. Maybe it's an extra motivation for the grocer? It would make him even more likely to try to poison a yankee blanket manufacturer.

BRONIAN. But would a southern bigot fall in love with a Chinese laundress?

ALISON. *Somebody* has to wash his white sheet!

(*RORY and ANDREW enter from kitchen. ANDREW is munching on a sandwich.*)

RORY. Did you get Andrew a room yet?

BRONIAN. Annabel's fixing it up in the bedroom.

ANDREW. I should warn you—I snore.

BRONIAN. I mean. . . .

ALISON. (*interrupting*) Say! Why *can't* Andrew stay here, Bronian? You could work on the script without even having to get out of your pajamas.

RORY. Any new notions on the script?

ALISON. Well, besides the pogo stick and the Chinese laundress, we now have a bigoted grocer. Of course we've barely scratched the surface.

BRONIAN. We still need a character with a dark secret to conceal, a creepy stranger who goes around saying obliquely mysterious things which upset the other players, and I'm having a hell of a time deciding which member of the family will be the vicious dope peddler.

ANDREW. Hey, now, just a minute—!

RORY. How about the wastrel son? The family treats him with contempt, so pushing dope is his revenge against society.

ANDREW. Olivia is an only child! How can there be a wastrel son?

ALISON. Maybe she's schizophrenic?

BRONIAN. It's easy to work *in*. . . !

ANNABEL. (*leans head in from bedroom*) Andrew, do you know anything at all about teeth?

ANDREW. Brush three times daily and visit the dentist twice a year, avoid sugary snacks, floss when you brush—

ANNABEL. (*interrupting his spiel*) Never mind. I'll try a few more hotels. (*vanishes again*)

ALISON. Bronian, before Annabel gets a cauliflower ear — what *about* having Andrew stay here?

BRONIAN. We'd just get in each other's way.

ALISON. *Think!* If he stays here there won't be any hotel bills.

RORY. Not to mention restaurant meals and transportation.

ANDREW. You make it sound as if he's short on cash. . . ?

ALISON. Oh don't be silly, Andrew! A successful Broadway producer is *never* short on cash.

ANDREW. That's what *worries* me!

ANNABEL. (*entering from bedroom*) I don't know how many dentists have deserted their home towns for this convention, but I wish I had a few shares of stock in an aspirin company tonight!

BRONIAN. No luck? Well, I guess Andrew *will* have to stay here.

ANNABEL. Oh there are still a few places I can try. I just took a break to let my ear unflatten.

BRONIAN. You look exhausted. Why don't you go home and let Andrew get to work!?

ANDREW. And that's another thing! You said *I* could make the alterations. You gave me your solemn word. So *what's* all this about a bigoted grocer?

BRONIAN. Did I order you to change a *single word?* It's not *my* fault if you eavesdrop on a private conversation! Do it any way you want. You'll find a typewriter and some paper in the bedroom closet.

ANDREW. *You're* leaving, too?

BRONIAN. I'm taking Miss Blair home. We have things to talk over.

RORY. I'll take Annabel.

ALISON. First draw us a map so we can find Bronian's car.

RORY. It's easier to show you. It's right on our way to the subway.

ANNABEL. *Subway?* (*to BRONIAN*) Sure your budget can *afford* it?

BRONIAN. No. (*As ANDREW reacts, PHONE starts ringing.*) Ah! There's your mortician boss now! Start thinking sick!

ANDREW. I'll *never* sound convincing! (*PHONE rings again; he starts for it, OTHERS start toward hall door.*)

ALISON. Bronian, we can't go till you've told Andrew the new title!

ANDREW. (*picks up phone*) Hello. . . ? Yes, operator, this is he . . . (*As he waits for his party:*) I feel like a rat.

ANNABEL. Oh, what's one little lie between friends?!

ANDREW. (*gets his party*) Hi! How are you? . . . That's good . . . Yes, I'm in New York, all right.

RORY. Up to his *ears!*

(*OTHERS are all at hall door, now ready to depart.*)

ANDREW. (*on phone*) But you see, there's—uh—a sort of problem . . .

ALISON. Bronian, tell the man the new *title*—!

BRONIAN. I can't while he's on the phone!

ALISON. Well, at *least* tell *me!*

ANDREW. (*on phone*) Well—it's just that—I'm—how can I put this—? . . .

BRONIAN. (*to ALISON*) Baby, *this* title will have them lined up for tickets around the *block!*

ANDREW. (*on phone, but half-listening to BRONIAN*) It's just that I—that I—. . .

ALISON. (*to BRONIAN*) So what *is* it?

BRONIAN. (*a grandiloquent pronouncement:*) "THE GRITS OF WRATH"!

ANDREW. (*on phone, in stunned reaction to title, as OTHERS exit into hall:*) I have never been so sick in my entire life! . . . (*And as he stands there, still on phone, in numb shock—*)

THE CURTAIN FALLS

ACT TWO

BRONIAN's apartment. About 10 o'clock the following morning. The room is bright with sunlight spilling in from the patio. ANDREW is seen at the dinette table at curtain-rise, typing busily, manuscript paper here and there on the table, and an empty brandy glass. He finally stops typing, yanks the paper out of the typewriter with an air of finality, and places it atop a stack of pages. He leans back, stretches, yawns. Looks out window at sunlight in some surprise, consults his watch, shakes his head wearily, stands, and stretches again. He takes empty glass across to the bar, tilts the brandy bottle over it, but nothing comes out. He stoops out of sight behind bar with empty bottle. BRONIAN enters from bedroom, in robe and pajamas, hair mussed, bleary as before. He crosses groggily into kitchen. ANDREW rises with fresh bottle, uncaps it, pours a stiff shot, then—scratching his ribs with free hand—takes the drink and strolls out onto the terrace. He goes to parapet, sets glass on it, steps back, stretches and takes deep breath, then begins to do exercises—touching right hand to left shoe, reversing, etc.—facing away from room. BRONIAN enters with cup of coffee, which is clattering against the saucer, reacts to blinding sunlight. Outside, ANDREW pauses, takes a swallow of his drink, starts a new exercise. BRONIAN, without looking out onto patio, draws drapes shut. Room dims to non-blinding brightness. BRONIAN sips coffee, blinks himself a bit more awake, sees stacked manuscript on table, takes it down to upstage armchair, sets coffee on hassock, starts to read, fighting grogginess. Doorbell rings. BRONIAN sets manuscript beside coffee, goes to answer door. FRIEDA NEB-

43

COTT enters, a woman of determination and purpose, with a thin veneer of charm and good manners, attractive in a severe businesslike way.

FRIEDA. Bronian, aren't you even dressed?!

BRONIAN. I forgot to set my alarm. Sit down, Frieda . . . won't be a minute. (*starts for bedroom, stops, turns*) You didn't see anything of a mild-mannered youth in a pink turtleneck did you?

FRIEDA. No. But I had other things on my mind this morning. (*sits in upstage armchair, sees manuscript and coffee*) I note that oversleeping didn't prevent you from attending to business.

BRONIAN. I just sat down when you rang. (*starts for bedroom again*) What brings you here at this hour? (*exits*)

FRIEDA. (*picking up new-typed manuscript, pages through as she speaks*) Today's the first read-through, isn't it? After the plug I gave you in my column, I thought I'd drop by and drown my doubts.

BRONIAN. (*off*) What doubts? Didn't I read you the whole damned script the other night?!

FRIEDA. I wanted to be sure it *was* the script and not just your tortured improvisation. (*pause*) Bronian, what's this I'm reading? I don't remember anything about a vicar.

BRONIAN. (*leans out of bedroom in half-buttoned shirt, fixing tie*) *Is* there a vicar? I haven't read the re-writes yet. (*He goes back into bedroom.*)

FRIEDA. Bronian, these lines haven't been re-written, they've been replaced! There's barely a *hint* of the plot-line remaining!

BRONIAN. (*from off . . . beat . . . then:*) . . . Would you say the change was for the better . . . or worse. . . ?

(*FRIEDA, an odd—almost furtive—look on her face, glances swiftly at the bedroom, then pages rapidly, stops, looks, seems very pleased, then hastily shuts script and:*)

FRIEDA. Better. Much, much better! You have a rare find in Andrew Kimmer. By the way, when do I meet him?

BRONIAN. (*still off*) As soon as I find him myself!

FRIEDA. Is he the pink turtleneck? (*BRONIAN enters buttoning his suit jacket.*) When did you lose him?

BRONIAN. When I got up. I heard him typing as I climbed out of bed. He can't have gotten far.

FRIEDA. Nobody passed me in the hall, is there a back way out?

BRONIAN. A service elevator off the kitchen, but Andrew wouldn't know about it. And why would he go out the rear if he did? (*takes manuscript from her*) Let me see the part about the vicar . . . (*scans page*) Say—this *is* different, isn't it!

FRIEDA. Startlingly so! There's a world of difference between a shy country grocer and a sex-crazed prelate! And where in the world did he dig up the Chinese laundress!?

BRONIAN. She's *in?!* I thought Andrew was joking!

FRIEDA. Bronian—why? *Noblesse Oblige,* in its own way, was a fine play. Even if this re-write is splendid— why re-write at all?

BRONIAN. It's play-production, Frieda. Change is the name of the game. When author, director and cast get together, something electric takes over and changes just . . . happen.

FRIEDA. If the playwright allows them to happen.

BRONIAN. (*laughingly*) They usually do. You see . . .
no matter how ludicrous on the surface, no matter how
self-serving any suggestion may be, the one great un-
derlying truth that we all know is that everybody is dedi-
cated to making it a great show. If it's already great,
then to make it better.

FRIEDA. But couldn't too much tampering also make
it worse?

BRONIAN. Of course it could. But the enthusiasm is
contagious and the playwright catches it too. All the tur-
moil makes him see new possibilities and then we're off
and running.

FRIEDA. (*rises*) Speaking of which . . . we'd better
hurry. I have a broadcast to tape this morning and we
only have about an hour. I must rescue you, dear boy.

BRONIAN. Forgive my failing memory. Are we going
someplace? And rescue me from what?

FRIEDA. Alison Blair! (*BRONIAN looks up, incredulous.*) All things considered, it might be better if you
decided she was *not,* after all, right for the part.

BRONIAN. *Which* part?

FRIEDA. Then she's not *definite* yet!

BRONIAN. Not the precise *role,* but she certainly gets a
part.

FRIEDA. I *don't* think so.

BRONIAN. Well, think again! (*Unnoticed by either of
them, ANDREW enters between the drawn drapes,
starts for bar with now-empty glass, sees the two of
them and stops, listening.*) And what's this "all things
considered"?! Which things?

FRIEDA. If it has escaped your notice — and it probably
has — Alison Blair is slightly nuts over you.

BRONIAN. (*startled, but not displeased*) You're crazy.
We work well together — we've had a few laughs — but
that's all there is to it.

FRIEDA. You don't listen carefully. I said *she* was nuts over *you*. Those things are contagious. Whatever feelings you *don't* think you have for her, if she knows her strategy she can make you *think* you think so. I don't want her around you any more. You have too many weak moments.

BRONIAN. You'll be sorry to hear this isn't one of them. Alison gets a part, or— (*sees ANDREW*) Oh. There you are.

FRIEDA. (*follows his gaze*) And how long have *you* been on the party line, Mr. Kimmer?

ANDREW. You know who I am?

FRIEDA. I recognized the shirt.

ANDREW. News travels fast in this town. What's this about Alison and the play?

FRIEDA. That is a private matter between Bronian and myself.

ANDREW. Not while I have cast-approval, it's not. Mr. Pendrick—

BRONIAN. It's nothing, Andrew, nothing. Just a notion Frieda had.

FRIEDA. (*half-starts toward foyer*) We'll talk about *that* on our way to City Hall.

BRONIAN. Who's going to City Hall?!

FRIEDA. We are. To take out a marriage license.

ANDREW. I'd say "Congratulations!" but I can see Mr. Pendrick's face.

BRONIAN. Frieda, is this some kind of joke?

FRIEDA. Your bewilderment is wonderfully convincing, Bronian. However, I *do* have the tape-recording of your proposal. *And* two witnesses.

BRONIAN. (*with no self-assurance*) You've got to be kidding!

FRIEDA. Are you trying to tell me you don't remember?

BRONIAN. I *am* telling you. I distinctly recall *not* proposing to you.

FRIEDA. Max and Ernestine recall differently.

BRONIAN. Your business manager and your secretary, if you asked them, would recall your shooting Archduke Ferdinand!

FRIEDA. Would you like to hear the tape? Or perhaps you'd like to hear me play it on my one o'clock broadcast! Bronian Pendrick, do you mean to tell me you deliberately pretended to make me an offer of marriage just for the sake of getting a plug in my newspaper column?!

BRONIAN. Frieda—Listen—I've got to think about this. Yesterday is sort of blurry. If I somehow gave you the impression—

FRIEDA. Impression? Down on one knee, slipping a ring onto my finger? (*flashes ring at him*) You call that *somehow?!*

ANDREW. She probably had the magic moment recorded on film, too!

FRIEDA. Perhaps I should have!

BRONIAN. Damn it, Frieda, I couldn't have proposed to you. I don't love you.

FRIEDA. That's not what you said that night. You were exceedingly attentive, highly emotional and impeccably romantic!

ANDREW. How romantic can you get in front of two witnesses?

BRONIAN. Hey, that's right! I'd never get romantic in front of witnesses!

FRIEDA. Ah, then you're *not* sure about that night! Are you! *Are* you!

BRONIAN. L-look . . . I— I can't possibly marry you—I can't possibly marry *anybody* until I have a hit show going again. If everything goes well, Frieda, perhaps we can talk this over . . .

FRIEDA. With Alison Blair flaunting herself at you through four weeks of intensive rehearsal, you are quite capable of making sure things did *not* go well!

BRONIAN. You think I'd scuttle my own show?!

FRIEDA. I simply want temptation out of your way. It makes the outcome likelier.

ANDREW. Mr. Pendrick, either Alison is in my show or there is no show! (*sits, folds arms defiantly*)

FRIEDA. If she stays *in,* my claws come *out! Nobody* has a hit show in this town unless I want them to! When I got through with your show, Mr. Kimmer, there'd be a lynch mob waiting for you at the Peoria Airport.

ANDREW. I can always go home by train.

BRONIAN. Shut up! *Both of you!* Before you finish your tandem flamenco on my corpse, let me have a few last words. Andrew, I cannot afford to have you antagonize one of the most powerful columnists in the country. But on the other hand—if you'll stop that premature preening, Frieda?—anybody with half a brain knows that a producer cannot override the playwright on casting. The Dramatists Guild has seen to that! Obviously, even the most cretinous neanderthal would realize that I can not please both of you. So what do I do . . . You tell me!

FRIEDA. All right. I'll give this much respite: You have until six o'clock this evening to convince Sir Galahad here that Alison is out of the show, Bronian. If I haven't heard from you by that time, I will begin writing a column about you that will win the Pulitzer Prize for concentrated venom. You won't be able to produce a corner flea circus when I finish with you!

ANDREW. Ah! The Poison Pen school of journalism!

How effective! Amateurish, but effective!

(*As FRIEDA draws breath to reply doorbell rings.*)

BRONIAN. Saved by the bell! Back to your corners, you two! We've got company. (*Answers door: CHARLES CARPENTER enters.*) Oh! Good morning Charles.

CHARLES. (*sees FRIEDA approaching*) Well, hello there Miss Nebcott. . . !?

FRIEDA. (*as she passes BRONIAN*) I'll phone you no later than five minutes to six. (*exits right past CHARLES as if he weren't there.*)

CHARLES. Was it something I said?

BRONIAN. (*closing door*) Probably. (*goes to bar, fixes drink*)

ANDREW. (*rising to greet a bewildered CHARLES*) So you're Charles Carpenter. Up bright and early.

BRONIAN. Andrew Kimmer, Charles. Our playwright.

CHARLES. (*shakes ANDREW's hand automatically*) Happy to meet you. I've memorized half the grocer's lines already.

ANDREW. I'm sorry to hear that. The grocer has been deleted from the script.

BRONIAN. When did that happen?

ANDREW. About three-fifteen this morning. He got bumped off by a pogo stick.

BRONIAN. Then you *are* using it!

ANDREW. Anything to keep the audience's mind off the *title!*

CHARLES. I *like* the title. . . ?

ANDREW. Where were you when I needed you?

BRONIAN. Don't worry Charles. There's still a juicy role for you. (*looks at ANDREW*) Isn't there?

ANDREW. I think he'd fit the part of the vicar nicely. Of course, I can't be sure till I see him wrapped in a towel.

BRONIAN. (*about to sip drink, chokes*) Let me see that script.

ANDREW. (*starts toward bedroom*) I've made carbons. You can both look. I'm going to take a hot shower and catch up on my lost sleep.

BRONIAN. I've got some pajamas in the dresser.

ANDREW. Thanks. (*exits*)

CHARLES. (*listens to wristwatch*) What *time* is it?

BRONIAN. Andrew sleeps by day and works by night. Writers do their best work when it's dark out.

CHARLES. Is that a fact?

BRONIAN. Grab a carbon and let's find out.

(*BRONIAN gets script and sits in left armchair. CHARLES does same and sits on sofa, during:*)

CHARLES. When Frieda phones, will you please tell her I'm sorry for what I said?

BRONIAN. You don't look sorry.

CHARLES. I don't know what I said! . . . "Grits of Wrath"?! Have I got an improper script?

BRONIAN. I hope so! . . . Charles! What do you have at the top of page two?

CHARLES. (*scanning*) You mean the stage direction? . . . LETITIA CALHOUN descends the staircase clad only in a—? (*looks up, bemused*) I didn't know you could get a hairshirt in a strapless model.

BRONIAN. Never mind. I can see it's not a typing error . . . Wow! Did you get to the next stage direction?!

CHARLES. (*looks, then*) I wonder if Animal Talent Scouts *has* hyenas for rent?

BRONIAN. Don't worry about where we get it. Just learn to ride it.

CHARLES. (*turns page*) The zoo-keeper's certainly a

colorful character. Why does he wear a death's-head mask?

BRONIAN. Maybe to symbolize what happens if you get too close to the cages at feeding time. But I must say it goes nicely with his black hooded robe.

CHARLES. It just doesn't seem to jibe with the quiver of arrows on his back.

BRONIAN. There's a clue on the bottom of the page, where you give the sermon on Greed to the daughter. It says she has a target painted on the stomach of her kimono.

CHARLES. Oh, I see it — But — That's strange . . . She's supposed to keep that target covered at all times with her rice bowl. What rice bowl?

BRONIAN. Even laundresses have to eat! (*Doorbell rings; BRONIAN gets door; RORY enters, intensely curious.*)

RORY. Hey, I just passed Frieda Nebcott in the lobby, and she looked as happy as Hamlet's insurance man! What —? Oh, hi Charles.

BRONIAN. She'll calm down.

CHARLES. Hi Rory.

BRONIAN. — I hope.

RORY. Before or after her next column?

BRONIAN. Don't worry about her column. Worry about her one o'clock broadcast! Although she did offer an armistice till six.

CHARLES. If I could only remember what I said!

RORY. A fight? Those two? No sign of blood. . . ?

CHARLES. I wouldn't hit a woman.

RORY. I didn't mean on her! . . . But *you* look reasonably fit, too! Bronian. . . ?

BRONIAN. I only audited the match. Frieda went a few rounds with the Peoria kid.

RORY. Where's he laid to rest?

BRONIAN. He handled himself quite nicely. He has an admirable command of vicious gentility.

RORY. And you didn't stop them?

BRONIAN. I was too busy rooting for him. He was defending my honor.

RORY. What the hell did Frieda want?

BRONIAN. Alison out of the cast.

RORY. She's crazy!

BRONIAN. That's what *I* said.

CHARLES. I still don't know what *I* said!

RORY. What *did he* say?

BRONIAN. "Hello there, Miss Nebcott."

RORY. What's wrong with that?

BRONIAN. He picked a bad time.

RORY. How far did Andrew get with the script?

BRONIAN. A lot farther than I expected. Maybe farther than I wanted.

RORY. Oh, listen. What I came about—Annabel thinks she can get one of the tapestries up at the Cloisters for the Calhoun mansion. Can I borrow your car to drive her up there?

BRONIAN. I don't know as how it will fit in with the new mood of the show now, Rory. Tell you what— (*grabs up manuscript*)—I'll come along with you and read this on the way. Then maybe I can help Annabel decide.

CHARLES. I thought we were going to have a read-through.

BRONIAN. We are. Look it over, and when Alison gets here, you two start without us.

RORY. Tell her we'll be back as soon as we can.

BRONIAN. (*as he and RORY head for the door*) Oh! And if anybody from Equity shows up to audition for the minor roles, read with them, will you?

RORY. I only posted the notice half an hour ago.

BRONIAN. There'll probably be a *few* coming by before we get back. Sorry for the haste, Charles. See ya!

(*BRONIAN and RORY exit. CHARLES settles back to read, frowns, looks around, sees drapes shut, goes upstage and opens them. Room brightens. He returns to chair, begins reading again. The telephone rings. He answers it.*)

CHARLES. Hello? . . . Oh yes, he is . . . But he's in bed . . . You *know* he's in bed? . . . Well—I suppose he can have visitors. It's a free country . . . Yes I'll tell him. . . . yes . . . okay . . . Bye. (*Hangs up phone, goes to bedroom door, knocks; when there is no response, he opens the door, and we hear the shower going; he hesitates, doorbell rings, he closes bedroom door, answers doorbell.*) Good morning Alison.

ALISON. (*enters from hall*) And how is the lovesick grocer this fine day?

CHARLES. You mean me?

ALISON. Unless you're reading for the Chinese Laundress. (*sees CHARLES's script, picks it up*) Well! Either Andrew worked all night, or he left a saucer of milk for the brownies.

CHARLES. He worked all night.

ALISON. (*certainly not needing this clarification*) Thank you. (*sits, begins paging through the script*) He must be the fastest typewriter in the midwest.

CHARLES. That reminds me—Who is V. Nelson Slomber?

ALISON. A Peoria undertaker, and how does fast typing remind you of that?

CHARLES. It wasn't the typing, it was the midwest.

ALISON. Why, Charles, darling, that makes *sense!* Have you been exercising or something?

CHARLES. (*pleased, but confused*) I—

ALISON. (*suddenly uneasy*) Wait a minute—Where did you hear that name?

CHARLES. There was a phone call just before you came in, and—By the way, Andrew can have visitors, can't he? I said he could.

ALISON. Holy crow! Where is he?!

CHARLES. (*gestures at bedroom*) In there—(*ALISON charges into bedroom; we hear her scream; she pops right out again, slams door, leans back against it with her eyes closed in chagrin as CHARLES finishes, unhappily:*)—taking a shower.

ALISON. (*pauses a beat*) He's finished. (*opens eyes, sighs, steps away from door shaking her head sadly*)

CHARLES. I didn't expect you to dash right in.

ALISON. Neither did he.

(*ANDREW enters, tousle-haired, in BRONIAN's robe, clutching it shut.*)

ANDREW. The bathroom's free.

ALISON. (*her back to him*) Thank you, Abraham Lincoln. (*turns*) I didn't mean to barge in that way.

ANDREW. I thought you barged in very nicely.

ALISON. I wasn't trying to get to the bathroom, however.

CHARLES. Where did you think he was taking that shower?

ANDREW. You wanted to see me take a shower?

ALISON. Some other time. Andrew, your boss is coming to visit you.

CHARLES. He is?

ALISON. That's what you *told* me. . . !

CHARLES. Oh. You mean V. Nelson Slomber is Andrew's boss!

ANDREW. My boss is coming *here?*

CHARLES. I said *you* were here . . . I had no idea you were a fugitive. That's the second time today I said the wrong thing.

ANDREW. Oh, you can forget about Frieda Nebcott, for pete's sake. You didn't say a thing to offend her.

ALISON. And who *would?!*

ANDREW. You're looking at him. I've got to get out of here.

ALISON. No one escapes the wrath of Frieda Nebcott.

ANDREW. I mean before my *boss* arrives. I don't *care* what *Frieda* thinks.

ALISON. Well you should. No matter what Frieda Nebcott does, you have to be kind to her if you want to work in the theatre.

ANDREW. She wanted you out of the show.

ALISON. I'll kill her. (*The doorbell rings.*)

ANDREW. It's Vicki!

ALISON. Who the hell is Vicki?

ANDREW. Vicki is the "V" in V. Nelson Slomber — MY BOSS!

ALISON. Your boss is a woman?

CHARLES. It was a woman who phoned here. That's why I got so confused.

ALISON. Now, Charles, don't go blaming your condition on a phone call. (*Doorbell rings again.*)

ANDREW. I've got to hide. Where can I hide?

ALISON. Why hide? She thinks you're sick in bed, doesn't she? So be sick in bed.

ANDREW. That's a good idea.

*(Dashes into bedroom, shuts door; ALISON answers
bell; VICKI enters; she may be a lady mortician,
but she is also a real dish.)*

VICKI. Good morning. I'm Vicki Slomber. I phoned a
few minutes ago from the bus station. Where is Andrew?

CHARLES. He's being sick in bed.

VICKI. What. . . ?

ALISON. May I introduce Charles Carpenter? If you
say "no," I'll understand.'

VICKI. Aren't you the gentleman I spoke with on the
phone? I thought you were Mr. Pendrick. (*to ALISON*)
Are you by any chance *Mrs.* Pendrick?

ALISON. Not even by design. I'm Alison Blair.

VICKI. Oh, of course! I should have recognized you.
But I've been so worried about Andrew—!

ALISON. That's perfectly all right. Would you like to
see him now?

VICKI. Thank you. You're very kind.

CHARLES. (*as they near the bedroom door*) Don't
forget to knock this time.

VICKI. What does he mean?

ALISON. Last time I walked right in, Andrew was—
uh—asleep, and I woke him.

CHARLES. In the shower?

ALISON. He wasn't *in* the shower!

VICKI. What?

CHARLES. Oh . . . OH! Now I see why he was so
upset.

VICKI. Upset? I don't understand.

ALISON. Good! (*knocks on door to forestall any more
discussion*) Andrew? Andrew, you have a visitor.
(*opens door gently*)

ANDREW. (*off, his voice at death's door*) Is it . . .Is it Vicki? . . . Charles said she was coming . . .

CHARLES. At the time, I had no idea his boss was a lady.

ALISON. (*quickly overriding this*) Yes, it's Vicki, Andrew. Shall I send her in?

ANDREW. (*off*) No, I'll be right out, as soon as I get a robe on.

VICKI. (*anxiously*) Do you think he should?

CHARLES. If he's not wearing pajamas.

ALISON. She means get out of bed! (*to VICKI*) He'll be all right. It's just a bad cold.

VICKI. It's so kind of Mr. Pendrick to let him stay here . . . By the way, where *is* Mr. Pendrick? I wanted to thank him.

ALISON. (*to CHARLES*) Yes, where is Bronian, anyhow?

CHARLES. I'm not sure. I was so worried about offending Frieda that I didn't pay close attention. He said something about going into a cloister.

ALISON. *Bronian?!*

CHARLES. *And* Rory. They were going to take Annabel with them.

ALISON. How ecumenical *is* this place?

(*ANDREW enters, his hair still tousled, trying his best to look deathly ill.*)

VICKI. Andrew! Come, sit down! Let me feel your forehead! (*She does so.*) You're dripping wet! Are you sure this isn't the flu?

ANDREW. (*sits in upper arm chair*) No, really, it's just a cold.

ALISON. Andrew, I can't get any sense out of Charles,

but that's par for the course. Do *you* know? What's this about Bronian going into a cloister?

ANDREW. (*startled*) Cloister? Good grief! He was upset, I know, about proposing, but I didn't think he'd do anything so drastic.

ALISON. Proposing to *whommmmmm?*

ANDREW. Apparently he's supposed to marry Frieda Nebcott.

VICKI. The columnist? How exciting!

ALISON. (*very shaken*) When did all *this* come about?

ANDREW. Some time last night, I think.

VICKI. I thought you were sick in bed last night?

ANDREW. Oh, I was. It was the night before last, on that date he had. When you work all night, your time-sense gets confused.

VICKI. *Who* worked all night?

ANDREW. (*realizing his slip*) Mr. Pendrick! He never stops working.

ALISON. (*in hurt anger*) Except to propose marriage!

CHARLES. *I* didn't know that.

ANDREW. Alison—In fairness to Bronian, I should tell you that he doesn't remember a thing about it.

ALISON. Then why is he going into a cloister?

CHARLES. He *did* say he'd be *back* . . .

ALISON. Well, *that* was a quickie calling! Charles . . . are you sure about that?—Oh what am I saying? Of course you're not sure! You're never sure about anything! Andrew, please, tell me about this proposal!

ANDREW. Frieda said she has two witnesses.

ALISON. I'll bet she does! (*sarcasm*) She probably keeps two witnesses with her at all times just in case. Well, who *are* these two witnesses? I want to get to the bottom of this.

ANDREW. She said Max and Ernestine. She also managed to get his proposal recorded on tape.

ALISON. I gotta hand it to her—she's vicious, but she's organized!

VICKI. *When* did all this happen?

ANDREW. Uh. This morning, when I woke up! I heard them shouting from in here.

ALISON. Max and Ernestine?!

ANDREW. Frieda and Mr. Pendrick. According to her, they were supposed to be going to get the license.

ALISON. Are you sure that's not where they are right now?

CHARLES. I don't think so. She said she'd call him not later than five minutes to six.

VICKI. Why five minutes to?

ANDREW. Because he had until six to make up his mind about Alison.

ALISON. (*hurt*) You mean he couldn't make it up right then and there?!

ANDREW. He did. Frieda simply wouldn't accept his decision. She said she'd ruin him if he didn't do things her way. I know he really wants you in the show. You could see it in his face.

VICKI. From the bedroom?

ANDREW. *I peeked out!* . . . Sorry, I didn't mean to shout. If you only knew how *much* I appreciate your coming all the way to New York to *see* me, Vicki!— What about the *funerals* you'll be losing?

VICKI. I'll catch up after Labor Day. The important thing is for you to get well. There are circles under your eyes. You need rest.

ALISON. What about you, Vicki? You must have been on the bus all night. (*picks up carbon of script, scribbles on top sheet as:*) My apartment's not far. If you need a place to stay, I've got plenty of room. Guard the phone number with your life, it's unlisted. (*hands script to VICKI, starts for door*)

ANDREW. Alison, you're not *going?*

ALISON. It'll be easier on all concerned if I leave right now. Tell Bronian—No, don't tell him anything. Just say I called and said I'd changed my mind about the part. (*exits to hall*)

ANDREW. Two days in show business, and I hate it already! (*heads for bedroom*) I've got to get some rest. Vicki—Why don't you take Alison up on her offer? Leave a copy of her number. I'll phone you later. (*exits*)

CHARLES. Here, I have a pencil.

VICKI. Thank you. (*about to copy number, double-takes at topsheet*) What is *this* script? I thought Mr. Pendrick was doing *Andrew's* play?

CHARLES. That *is* Andrew's play. He's made a few alterations.

VICKI. When? This is an entire script, and definitely *not* the one he had with him when he left Peoria! . . . There's something strange about all of this.

CHARLES. Alison said something about the brownies doing a rewrite. I thought she was kidding.

VICKI. (*paging through script*) The brain that concocted *this* wasn't much *bigger* than a brownie's! (*looks up, concerned*) Mr. Carpenter—Do you suppose the fever has affected his mind? He acted so peculiarly . . .

CHARLES. Everybody's acting peculiarly today. Even *I* noticed. First Frieda, then Bronian, now Alison and Andrew. I spent weeks developing the character of the country grocer, and now I'm a vicar who goes around wearing nothing but a towel!

VICKI. (*reacts*) I've got to *read* this thing!

CHARLES. So do I. Would you like to do it together? Alison's gone and I need a partner.

VICKI. Do you have any scenes with lady morticians?

CHARLES. It wouldn't surprise me. A man who can't work unless it's dark outside is capable of anything.

VICKI. (*feigning elaborate unconcern*) Yes, Andrew *does* have odd working habits . . . What time did he finish?

CHARLES. Let me see—I got here some time after eleven, and he was just going to bed. I remember thinking my watch had stopped.

VICKI. Funny coincidence. Just about eleven, I remember thinking that my circulation had stopped. Have you ever ridden the night bus from Peoria? I was so stooped over that when I held my hand out to flag down a cab, somebody dropped a quarter in it. If he'd only *told* me! What's so hard about saying, "The script needs work, and I'm going to stay a bit longer than planned!"? And to top it off. . . . (*lifts script in both hands and glares at it*) *This* script is worse than when it left the *mortuary!* What was wrong with the *original* version?

CHARLES. I guess grocers aren't *in,* this season.

VICKI. Two years' work, wrecked in a single night! What could Andrew have been thinking of? When I think of all the hours I spent re-typing for him. All the times I didn't fire him for falling asleep during a wake, or for oversleeping and missing funerals so that I had to go to the cemetery and cover up for him—!

(*BRONIAN, RORY and ANNABEL enter from hallway. ANNABEL throws herself wearily into upper armchair. RORY goes to sofa and flops on his back with an arm flung across his eyes, and BRONIAN goes right to the bar and pours himself a large drink, then notices VICKI.*)

BRONIAN. I beg your pardon, I didn't see you there. I'm Bronian Pendrick. (*takes big swallow of drink, winces it down and then approaches her*) Excuse my not being here when you arrived. Has she read yet, Charles?

CHARLES. We were about to, but she seemed unhappy about the script.

RORY. (*uncovers his eyes and sits up*) She's not the only one. Where the hell am I going to rent a hyena? And I can't think of one choreographer who'd be willing to stage a Penguin Ballet Dream Sequence. (*sees VICKI, stands*) Hi, I'm Rory Madden, the unhappy director.

VICKI. (*trying to cope with his earlier remark*) . . . A HYENA?!

RORY. I *could* try a large dog, but would it devour the bowl of carrion in Act Three?

ANNABEL. Couldn't we *fake* the carrion? You know, use chopped-up Gainesburgers or raw liver instead?

RORY. Nope! The stench is supposed to permeate the audience, row by row. Andrew thinks it will give the situation *subliminal* impact!

BRONIAN. I can see the headlines, now: "Come and see the show that is *supposed* to stink!"

ANNABEL. You gotta admit, it hasn't been done. If you can get a hyena—*and* get him to eat out of a bowl. . . .

RORY. Actually, getting the hyena's the easy part. My toughest job will be to make the vicar convincing when he wrestles the hyena for the carrion!

CHARLES. (*startled*) Who wins?

ANNABEL. That's entirely up to you. The act has an optional ending. If you win you marry the Chinese laundress. If you lose, the girl gets one of the zoo-keeper's arrows right through the rice bowl. Oh boy! Wait until you try to put Alison through *that* staging!

CHARLES. But Alison's not going to be *in* the show.

BRONIAN. Since when?

VICKI. (*quickly*) She *called!* She said she'd changed her mind.

CHARLES. And she looked terribly upset.

ANNABEL. Did she say that, *too?*

CHARLES. No, just said to say she'd called, and rushed right out.

BRONIAN/RORY. (*look at one another one beat; then, in chorus:*) *Frieda!*

ANNABEL. She was here *again?*

VICKI. Not exactly. But her name came up, and. . . .

BRONIAN. Alison's gorge came right after it! She should have waited for me.

CHARLES. There was some confusion in her mind as to your whereabouts.

RORY. Three guesses where the confusion began!

CHARLES. (*quite meekly, to himself*) Oh dear! Have I done it again?

ANNABEL. Charles, where *did* you say Bronian had gone?

VICKI. He didn't say for sure. Something about a monastery . . .?

BRONIAN. Charles, you are an imbecile! I've got to talk to her! If I only knew where she lived.

ANNABEL. I thought you took her home last night?

BRONIAN. Sure! To the Graymore! That place is bigger than the Plaza! I'd have to pound on half a hundred doors to find her—if she were in—and if I could get past Attila the Doorman.

RORY. You should have seen her to her room. Or didn't you trust yourself?

BRONIAN. *She* didn't trust myself.

ANNABEL. Hey! Wait a minute!—you told me this morning you were out till all hours. If you dropped Alison at her apartment building door—where were you after that?

BRONIAN. I'm damned if I know! Probably dozed off in the cab and went sleepwalking again.

RORY. Say, Bronian, I know this might sound silly but . . . sleepwalkers don't remember things usually, and you don't remember proposing to Frieda . . . is it possible that. . . ?

BRONIAN. STOP! Don't even *think* that! Sleepwalkers are walking dreamers. They are supposed to be acting out subconscious desires. If I thought I subconsciously *wanted* to marry that typing harpy I'd *kill* myself!

VICKI. Does Frieda Nebcott *know* you walk in your sleep, Mr. Pendrick?

BRONIAN. I hope not! She has enough on me already.

ANNABEL. You know, I'm suspicious about her recording your marriage proposal . . . but I don't know *why*, exactly.

VICKI. *I* have a clue: How could she *know?*

RORY. How could she know *what?*

VICKI. Well, aren't marriage proposals generally *impromptu?*

ANNABEL. (*realizes*) Hell, *yes!* Frieda wouldn't tote a live mike around *just in case*, Bronian!

CHARLES. You mean . . . she'd have had no way of knowing he was *going* to propose.

ANNABEL. There! Even *Charles* smells a rat! That *proves* there's something fishy!

BRONIAN. If I could only remember!

VICKI. Then you're not *sure* if you proposed or not?

BRONIAN. My every instinct tells me No No No, but my memory . . . Hey, how the hell did *you* get into my personal life?

VICKI. Nobody told me this was a *private* panic.

CHARLES. A new brain might come in *handy*.

ANNABEL. We're discussing *Bronian*'s problem.

VICKI. Mr. Pendrick—What if you proposed while she was taping her show, and she didn't realize she had the recording of it till later?

BRONIAN. She *did* make a threat to broadcast it. . . !

RORY. Sure! I'll bet that's what happened. And Max and Ernestine just happened to walk in by accident.

BRONIAN. But—*Marriage* to *Frieda?* Asleep, awake or dead, I'd *never* propose to that fourth estate Frankenstein! Besides, everybody *knows* the way I feel about *Alison!*

VICKI. Including Frieda Nebcott?

BRONIAN. Especially including Frieda Nebcott. Alison should only feel the feeling for me as strongly as Nebcott does.

VICKI. Well then! What if you sleepwalked, and Frieda met you and knew you were asleep, and instead of identifying herself as Frieda. . . .

RORY. Pretended she was Alison! Bronian . . . It's just possible.

ANNABEL. And it's just the sort of underhanded trick that ink-stained wretch would love.

BRONIAN. But wouldn't I mention Alison by name? I mean during the proposal? That would bollix up her recording wouldn't it?

ANNABEL. You may have just called her "darling"! A proposing man doesn't always use his beloved's *name.*

RORY. Hey . . . if that's true—then that puts the squelch on the whole scheme. Don't you see, Bronian? If you never mention your beloved's *name* on the tape, what's Frieda *got?*

VICKI. Just a proposal *by* Mr. Pendrick, but not *to* anybody!

BRONIAN. All she can prove is I'm in *love,* but not with *whom!* She can't even prove that's *me* on her tape!

CHARLES. Then who *did* propose to her? (*All stare at him.*) . . . I was only trying to follow the plot.

ANNABEL. Maybe if he wrote things down, he'd get them straight. . . ?

CHARLES. I'll do anything I can. (*finds paper and pencil during:*)

BRONIAN. I've got to hear that tape. It's the only way I'll ever find out the truth.

VICKI. Before you do, you're going to have to get back in her good graces in the matter of Alison Blair.

RORY. That's right! Frieda won't come *near* you as long as she thinks you're retaining *Alison* in the show! Convince her Alison's out and Frieda will fly through that door and into your arms. (*CHARLES has unearthed writing materials and sits poised to write.*)

BRONIAN. (*strides quickly to the door and locks it*) I'd like to see her try it! (*CHARLES nods happily and writes that down.*)

ANNABEL. But Frieda won't believe Alison's *out* of the show unless someone else is *in*.

VICKI. What about *me!?* You'd have a tough time finding a *regular* actress who'd pretend to have the lead in a show, but *Frieda* doesn't have to know who I am!

BRONIAN. But *I* sure as hell do. Who *are* you?

VICKI. I'm Vicki Slomber. Andrew's boss from Peoria. I came as soon as I heard he was sick.

BRONIAN. Sick?! Good heavens, why didn't somebody tell me?

ANNABEL. Uh, Bronian . . .

BRONIAN. Where is he? How is he? When did he . . . What's the mat—oh. Oh yeah. . . ! It all comes back to me *now*.

VICKI. (*dryly*) Now that it's *too late*.

RORY. (*to VICKI*) I suppose *Andrew* is going to be your next customer?

VICKI. There was a moment there when I felt that way, but—Now I know what happened to him. *You* happened to him—*all* of you.

BRONIAN. I don't get you.

VICKI. You're all so frenzied, so afraid, so helpless. Anyone with half a heart would do anything he could to please you. You give the impression that if life doesn't go the way you want it to every single second you'll all sit right down and sob yourselves sick. You take every little setback so tragically. . . !

ANNABEL. Dramatizing is our business.

VICKI. Well, helping people cope with misfortune is mine. Why don't you tell Frieda you've got a *new* girl in the role and take it from there?

BRONIAN. That's very kind of you, but what about your *undertaking* customers?

VICKI. They'll keep. I want Andrew to have his chance, and getting Alison into the show seems to be what he wants. So. . . ?

BRONIAN. It's perfect! We use *you* all during rehearsals, *and* out-of-town tryouts, but we secretly rehearse *Alison* in the role. Then on opening night, just before curtain. . . !

RORY. The star gets sick . . .

ANNABEL. But the show must go on. . . .

VICKI. And in the brave tradition of the theatre—

BRONIAN. —the understudy prepares to go on in the star's place. . . .

RORY. And the rest is show business history!

CHARLES. (*who has been busily writing*) I missed some of that. But it sounds like a great show. Whose is it?

BRONIAN. Andrew's, you numbskull! What did you *think* we were talking about?

RORY. Bronian, we've got to tell Alison *before* we tell Frieda!

ANNABEL. Ouch! He's right! If Frieda puts the item in her column before Alison knows what we're up to. . . !

BRONIAN. I'm going over there now and knock on every door in the Graymore until I find her.

VICKI. You don't have to do that. She gave me her room number. I'll swap you. *You* get the *number* if you'll help *me* find the *Graymore*. Alison's offered me her hospitality and I haven't slept in so long I'm not sure I remember *how!*

BRONIAN. I'll take you there myself! I want to tell Alison in person. Rory, you get on over to Equity and arrange a card for Miss Slomber. Annabel, you go see about renting that hyena; if Animal Talent Scouts can't provide one, try the Bronx Zoo.

CHARLES. (*as others head for front door*) But what about the reading?

BRONIAN. Can't you *pretend* there's a hyena here with you?! It's not as though he has to feed you *cues!* Wait till your stomach growls, then answer it!

(*BRONIAN, VICKI, RORY, and ANNABEL exit; CHARLES sits, sighs, opens his script, finds his place, waits. After a moment he prods his stomach. The TELEPHONE rings. CHARLES looks startled; starts to prod stomach again, TELEPHONE rings again. This time he realizes, answers:*)

CHARLES. Hello? . . . Oh hello Miss Nebcott! . . . Charles Carpenter . . . No, I'm sorry, he just left . . . Message? No there's no . . . oh, hold on . . . (*He consults his notes.*) There may be something here. I was told to write it down . . . Yes! Mr. Pendrick said something about wanting you to fly into his arms . . . Up to? I'm not up to anything! We all heard (*The curtain is starting down slowly.*) him say it . . . *All* of us. Rory and Annabel and that undertaker they decided to use for Alison. . . . Alison Blair. . . . No I don't know any details, but Bronian was taking the undertaker over to Alison's when he left . . . Yes, he seemed to be in excellent spirits. . . . Well the undertaker said something about taking setbacks tragically and sobbing, but nobody acted that way. . . . You don't take *what?* . . . Oh, shorthand. (*speaks very slowly and clearly*) Certainly I'll talk slower. I don't mind. After all, what are friends for? . . .

CURTAIN IS DOWN

ACT THREE

BRONIAN's apartment. A few hours later. The sofa has been moved out onto the terrace, and faces directly into the room. Terrace doors are open and out of sight, drapes closed to outer edges of terrace-door frame, forming — with their matching valance — a proscenium around the doorway. Armchairs are upstage left, in area below pullcord, angled to face the terrace, cocktail table paralleling the front edge of their cushions before them. Hassock is against lower left wall, below kitchen entrance. In short, the room's furniture has been arranged to face the "stage" which the terrace-area now resembles. There are scripts, pencils and paper on table and on cocktail table. Phone is no longer on bar. RORY enters from kitchen, jacketless, tieless, sleeves rolled up, pencil behind ear, carrying ice-bucket. He places this below center of sofa, steps back to observe effect, checks script on cocktail table, looks again, nods as if satisfied. BRONIAN and ALISON enter from corridor. RORY sees them.

RORY. Hi! It's just about set up. We're going to have to imagine the sweeping staircase, for the time being. Where'd you leave Vicki?

ALISON. Taking a shower.

BRONIAN. She'll come over us as soon as she feels wide-awake again. Is there any coffee? My stamina is starting to fray.

RORY. In the kitchen.

ALISON. Where's Charles? (*picks up script, strolls toward terrace*)

RORY. No idea. When I got back from Equity, he was gone.

71

BRONIAN. Where do you suppose he went? He *knows* there's a rehearsal!

ALISON. (*lounging back onto sofa to read script*) Are you sure? Nobody acted very rehearsal-minded all the time he was here. He may think the whole thing's off.

BRONIAN. After Frieda's broadcast, he may be right. What time is it, anyhow?

RORY. Relax. There's plenty of time to tune her in.

ALISON. Bronian, I wouldn't worry so much about that taped proposal. You can always claim you were on LSD or something.

BRONIAN. That may save my neck from the marital noose, but it'll never salvage my show. After the rave she gave us in her column, yesterday, I urged all my backers to tune her *in,* today! They'll be hanging on her every word — or *I* will!

RORY. All they'll find out is that you're engaged.

BRONIAN. But if Frieda follows the proposal-tape with an announcement of my *later* attempts to *renege* on the deal — !

ALISON. I guess it *would* be hard for them to entrust their money to a man who'd cheat his own fiancee! . . . You know, it's *hot* out here!

RORY. Well, the action does take place in the deep south.

ALISON. It's the only part of the original script Andrew didn't change. Wonder how he missed it?

BRONIAN. He had to leave it in. Who'd believe a hyena in a cold climate?

RORY. We could always supply the mysterious zoo keeper with *flaming* arrows.

ALISON. Stop it! That's my unfavorite scene in the whole play. I'm either going to have to teach Charles to like carrion, or check the Sears catalogue for steel rice bowls.

BRONIAN. We're going to *fake* the arrow shot, Alison.

ALISON. Great Godfrey, I should *hope* so! Assuming you *do* decide on flaming arrows, where's the fire escape in this place?

BRONIAN. I'm told the artificial ivy on the outside wall will support the weight of an average adult.

ALISON. (*sits up on sofa, looks up toward right beyond terrace wall*) *That* stuff? It looks as strong as brass tinsel after a heavy rain. And about as pretty.

BRONIAN. I didn't select this building for its architectural marvels.

ALISON. (*settles back again to read*) You got your money's worth.

BRONIAN. Rory, has Frieda called since you got back?

RORY. No. I thought *you* were supposed to call *her*.

BRONIAN. I would if I knew what to say that wouldn't torpedo all of us. Let's put on the broadcast.

RORY. (*goes to radio on highboy*) We've still got a few minutes. I'll tune in the station.

(*Doorbell rings. RORY fiddles with radio dials. BRO-NIAN gets door. ANNABEL enters carrying a large stuffed vulture.*)

ANNABEL. Ask me why I don't just get a parakeet like other people.

BRONIAN. What the hell is *that?!* I sent you for a hyena.

ANNABEL. Animal Talent Scouts nearly sent me for psychiatric examination. They have dogs, cats, birds, even a few chimps — but I guess there isn't much of a call for hyenas in this business.

RORY. You ever watch an act die on The Tonight Show?

ANNABEL. Well, anyhow, I was passing a taxidermist's shop and saw this in the window . . .

RORY. . . . and you couldn't resist it!

ANNABEL. . . . and I thought we might be able to use a viable alternative.

RORY. I'll bet the taxidermist kissed both your hands as he handed over the receipt. That's the most disgusting thing I've seen since I had lunch with the cast of ANIMAL HOUSE.

BRONIAN. How the hell is Charles supposed to ride a stuffed vulture?

RORY. We could use wires, *à la* Peter Pan . . . Charles could flap the wings with his knees.

ANNABEL. All right already! I'll take it back.

RORY. What makes you think that a taxidermist clever enough to get rid of that in the first place would be dumb enough to take it back?

ANNABEL. I made him give it to me on approval. You don't approve . . . so . . . But! Before I schlepp all the way back to Fourteenth Street let's check with the author. He may have had a change of heart about the hyena, too!

ALISON. (*still reading script*) The man who wrote this *has* no heart. Anyone who would inflict such a gruesome sight on a paying audience. . . !

RORY. You mean the vicar's hyena?

ALISON. I mean Charles Carpenter's *knees!* They knock together when he walks, and all the hair is worn off the inside of his legs.

BRONIAN. How do you know so much about Charles Carpenter's knees?

ALISON. I saw his Willy Loman in stock. Just before his son caught him with the floozie, his belt let go. I have to admit he brazened it out nicely in his lavender boxer shorts with his blue serge trousers dusting his shoes and the floor, with the floozie ad-libbing business about trying to get his clothes back in place, and his son standing there gaping in shock, while he coldly denied everything. One of the best comedy bits I ever saw.

ANNABEL. Arthur Miller meets Laurel and Hardy! . . . So . . . what about my vulture?

RORY. We can ask Andrew when he wakes up. I thought I'd let him keep snoring till we're ready to start.

ANNABEL. (*sets vulture on hassock . . . studies effect*) You know Bronian, if you had that dipped in bronze you could use it for a pop-art hat rack.

RORY. Or a pop art hat . . . shades of Hedda Hopper!

ALISON. (*sits up waving a sheet of paper*) Hey, I just solved the mystery of our missing actor! (*comes down to group*) I must have picked this up off the table with my script.

BRONIAN. (*takes paper and reads*) "I am sorry to be gone like this, but I didn't think Bronian would throw in the towel with the role. If I am going to be draped in black, which seems suitable for the role, I want to be sure it's *big* enough . . . "

ALISON. His best friend must have told him about his knees.

RORY. Charles' best friend is his dalmatian. Would a dog notice his master's knees?

ALISON. Well, they're pretty bony . . .

ANNABEL. Bronian, does he say when he'll be back?

BRONIAN. Uh . . . where was I? . . . "to make sure it's big enough to suit the temperament of a churchman. I'll see you all as soon as possible."

ANNABEL. Do they *sell* solid-black towels?

ALISON. They must. They sure couldn't *give* them away!

BRONIAN. Hey! Speaking of giving things away — What time is it?!

RORY. Oops! I'll get it! (*dashes to radio, turns it on*)

(*We hear THEME MUSIC; it fades; then:*)

FRIEDA. (*on radio*) Good afternoon. Today's show will be somewhat unusual, in that it is coming to you "live" and not pre-taped, as is my custom. What I am about to relate to you occurred so recently that there simply was not time before my broadcast to prepare anything but a few notes . . .

BRONIAN. (*sits on arm of lower armchair*) *And* an incriminating recording!

ALISON. Ssh!

FRIEDA. (*on radio*) Today, a shining light went out on old Broadway.

RORY. What *is* this — an open letter to Mayor Koch?

ANNABEL. (*sensing the metaphor*) Wait a minute — Listen!

FRIEDA. (*on radio*) There has passed from our midst a luminary whose aura truly glowed like the star she was — (*All react with sudden comprehension and intensified interest.*) — whose brilliance upon the stage will leave a darkness, indeed, in her wake. She was a young actress, far too young to have been taken from us so cruelly soon . . .

BRONIAN. But who? *Who?*

ANNABEL. She probably figures the suspense is good showmanship.

RORY. And she's right!

ALISON. Shh!

FRIEDA. (*on radio*) I was also privileged to know her as a dear, personal friend.

ALISON. Well, now we know it's not *me!*

OTHERS. *Ssh!*

FRIEDA. (*on radio*) The theatre, the world, and I, will never be quite the same without . . . Alison Blair. (*All ad-lib shock, cries of* "What?!", "Who?!", "Alison?", *etc., then crowd close to radio to hear more.*) As to the manner of her passing—I will not dwell upon it.

ALISON. Oh, *please* do! . . .

FRIEDA. (*on radio*) No matter how her passing came about, the tragedy would be the same. I—I cannot go on . . . The finger of death has touched too close to me . . .

BRONIAN. Not close *enough!*

FRIEDA. (*on radio*) So . . . just remember that Alison Blair is dead—

ALISON. (*with sardonic insight*) And that "you heard it here *first!*"

FRIEDA. (*on radio*) —and join with me in my silent, heartbroken sorrow. . . !

(*MUSIC comes up on radio; it is* Auld Lang Syne, *the GUY LOMBARDO rendition; ALISON covers her eyes with the palm of one hand.*)

ALISON. Wouldn't you know she'd find a way to end my obituary with "Happy New Year!"?!

(*RORY turns radio off, closes cabinet.*)

ANNABEL. You gotta admit—after *that* announcement, your "comeback" performance should be a sell-out!

ALISON. (*lurches toward sofa*) Excuse me, I've got to lie down!

RORY. You mean Frieda was *right?*

ALISON. Oh, *shut* up! (*flops on back on sofa*) You might show a little more respect for the dead.

BRONIAN. It could be worse. She might have announced our engagement.

ANNABEL. I can't understand it. Where did Frieda *get* such a notion?

RORY. "Notion?!" That was a sworn declaration! Do you suppose it's some kind of gag?

BRONIAN. A gag like that could ruin all of us, Frieda included. What do you think my backers will think of her integrity when they find out Alison's alive? Can they rely on her opinion of my *show* when she can't even tell if somebody's *breathing?!*

ALISON. How do you think *I* feel? The next friend I meet is going to die of heart failure! Worse than that, the bank has probably stopped payment on all my checks!

ANNABEL. I still want to know where Frieda *got* such an idea. . . ?

RORY. Oh, she's always had the *idea* of Alison kicking the bucket. Maybe it obsessed her until her mind snapped.

ALISON. What mind?! . . . Bronian, are you sure *you* didn't put this story into her head?

BRONIAN. Why would I tell her a thing like *that?*

ALISON. Well it would *certainly* ease her anxiety about my being in the *show!*

BRONIAN. We'll just have to wait till she phones and *ask* her.

ANNABEL. What if she phoned while you were gone?

RORY. I'm sure Charles would have mentioned it in his note—

ALISON. (*slowly, thoughtfully*) . . . Charles . . . You don't suppose. . . ?!

ANNABEL. But he knew you were alive. . . ? Of course —

RORY. Is anyone ever really sure just *what* Charles Carpenter does know?

ALISON. Oh, if he told Frieda I'm dead, I'll die . . . no, *he'll* die! I swear it!

BRONIAN. Save your strength. When Frieda learns you're alive, *she'll* kill him!

ALISON. This is ghastly! What am I going to do! All my friends are probably out ordering floral tributes!

ANNABEL. Now you'll find out who your *real* friends *are!* You'll forgive *me* if I don't send any?

BRONIAN. Hold it! Everybody! Listen — Maybe Alison being dead isn't so terrible after all.

ALISON. What are you going to do, rent me out to haunt houses?

BRONIAN. I'm going to *keep* you dead till opening night! Your appearance will be sensational!

RORY. How are you going to explain it to the audience? Everybody *knows* "the show must go on", but even the *Barrymores* knew where to draw the line!

BRONIAN. But don't you see — ? This is perfect! We *maintain* Frieda's credibility till my backers have put their *money* into the play, then we reveal Alison's existence to *undermine* everybody's credibility about that *marriage* proposal!

ALISON. And where do *I* while away the hours in the meantime? In a glass casket surrounded by sobbing dwarfs? In case it hasn't occurred to you, you're going to need a dead body to keep the rumor alive.

ANNABEL. Unless you want to fill an old urn with cigar ashes and tell everybody she returned to dust the time-saving way?

RORY. We may *all* wind up in the jug when the law hears we've been pulling the municipal coroner's leg!

BRONIAN. We? Why, Rory, *we* never said a *word* about Alison's death, did we? If Frieda wants to spread the tale, let *her* find the body if she can! We all continue to tell the world that, far as we know, Alison Blair is still vibrantly alive and well.

ALISON. And if that doesn't convince them, I pop up and vibrate for them! . . . Honestly, Bronian, this is crazy! I'll be damned if I hide out in this building till opening night, but I look like hell in a false beard!

(*Doorbell rings.*)

BRONIAN. That must be Charles! Now we can find out how much he knows!

ANNABEL. And write it on a postage stamp.

ALISON. Let me see that stupid note! (*takes it from BRONIAN*) If Frieda phoned, he'd surely have said *something—*!

(*RORY has answered door; VICKI enters, looking bright and alert.*)

VICKI. Hello, everybody! Rory, did you get me that Equity card?

RORY. Oh, yeah! Almost forgot about it. (*fumbles in pocket*) Here. Hope you like it.

VICKI. (*looks at it*) I don't understand. Who is "Charlotte Carstairs"?

RORY. That's your stage name. I thought it'd look good on a marquee with Charles Carpenter.

ALISON. (*back on sofa, scanning note*) Just beneath "The Late Alison Blair".

VICKI. They won't put *both* names up the *same night,* will they? I thought the idea was for nobody to know you were going on until I "got sick". If *your* name's there, won't they *suspect* something?

RORY. Only that we've lost our minds.

ANNABEL. Of course, we could always pretend she was appearing as a *prop!*

VICKI. I'm afraid I *still* don't understand . . . ?

BRONIAN. As a matter of fact, *we* don't quite get it, ourselves. You see — (*Doorbell rings.*) Ah! Here's the man who can straighten the whole thing out!

ALISON. If he's the rat responsible, *I* may just straighten *him* out — with a left hook!

BRONIAN. (*moves toward her, placatingly*) Now, now, Alison. Give the guy a break. You *know* how Charles is! And he *may* have done us a big *favor!*

(*VICKI has gone to door; as she opens it, FRIEDA enters foyer.*)

VICKI. Why, hello! You're Frieda Nebcott, the columnist, aren't you!

(*Others react with panic, instantly; there's only one thing to do: BRONIAN grabs pull-cord and closes drapes before ALISON, masking the terrace from view; the room dims considerably, as a result.*)

FRIEDA. Yes, but I don't believe I've seen *you,* before . . . ? Are you with the show?

VICKI. Uh . . . If Mr. Pendrick will *have* me, of course. I'm . . . uh . . . I'm — Charlotte Carstairs!

(*FRIEDA has now made her way around VICKI in*

foyer, and as she steps into room, BRONIAN— who until this moment has stood frozen before drapes with equally unsettled RORY and ANNA- BEL—comes down with the hollow heartiness of a used-car salesman.)

BRONIAN. Frieda! How wonderful to see you! You're looking splendid!

FRIEDA. How can you tell, in this midnight grotto? Why are your drapes closed? It's stifling in here! (*starts toward them*)

RORY. (*steps before her*) No! I mean—We want it this way. Dark and stifling.

FRIEDA. For heaven's sake, *why?* It's easily ninety degrees in here!

ANNABEL. We're in *mourning!*

BRONIAN. *Yes!* Deep mourning! Your broadcast came as quite a shock!

FRIEDA. Shock? But—Didn't you *know?!* Charles said *you* were the one who went over there with the *undertaker . . .* !?

BRONIAN. He—? Oh! Yes! That's right. I forgot.

FRIEDA. *Forgot?!*

ANNABEL. It was the shock. Blotted the whole thing out of his mind till your broadcast reminded him.

VICKI. Of what? What's happened? Oh! It's *Andrew!* Where is he? (*starts for bedroom*)

RORY. (*catches her arm*) Worse than that, "Charlotte"—It's Alison! She's . . . gone.

VICKI. Gone? But I just saw—!?

BRONIAN. We *all* feel that way—Here today, gone tomorrow.

ANNABEL. Her death was *very* sudden.

VICKI. *I'll* say it was!

FRIEDA. Annabel . . . How did she die?

BRONIAN. Don't *you* know?

FRIEDA. Charles was a bit garbled on the phone. I suppose his mind was shaken up.

ANNABEL. That happened the day he was born. The doctor slapped the wrong end.

VICKI. Look, I must be a little slow. What's this about Alison being dead, some kind of gag?

FRIEDA. Haven't you told her?

BRONIAN. We didn't want the child to feel she was stepping into a dead woman's shoes.

(*As all GROUP downstage, a rumpled, pajama-clad ANDREW enters unnoticed from bedroom, groggily scratching head, moving toward kitchen; he sees GROUP, pauses, squints at them in semi-gloom, looks for source of darkness, starts for drape-cord.*)

FRIEDA. A delayed shock is still a shock. You'd better tell her everything.

BRONIAN. I don't *know* everything!

VICKI. *I* don't know *anything!*

(*ANDREW, still unnoticed by GROUP, opens drapes; room brightens instantly, and we—but nobody else—see a startled ALISON standing there, trapped; there is only one thing to do, and she does it: she flops instantly onto her back on the sofa, crosses her hands over her breast, and goes shut-eyed and rigid just as the downstage GROUP turns to see where the light is coming from; FRIEDA, of course, gives a wild shriek of horror, recoiling into RORY's arms.*)

FRIEDA. It's Alison! Look! *It's Alison!* What's she doing there?!

ANDREW. (*bleary-eyed, looks*) She doesn't seem to be doing *anything* . . . (*yawns, stretches*) What's all the shouting about?

VICKI. That's what *I'd* like to know!

FRIEDA. Charlotte seemed to think it was *you*. But it's not. It's Alison.

ANDREW. (*looks at ALISON again*) Charlotte needs her eyes examined. (*looks back at GROUP*) Whoever *she* is.

VICKI. *I'm* Charlotte. Charlotte Carstairs. How do you do?

FRIEDA. You haven't met? Then why were you so excited? When you thought it was *Andrew* who'd died, you—

VICKI. How would *you* feel if the author of the play that was going to skyrocket you to stardom *died?!*

ANDREW. The author that could skyrocket *Frieda* to stardom hasn't been *born!*

BRONIAN. Now, now, Andrew! Can't we forget petty quarrels in the face of a great tragedy?

ANDREW. What great tragedy?

ANNABEL. (*to RORY, desperately*) Rory—I think I'm going to faint!

RORY. (*straightens FRIEDA, holds out arms to ANNABEL*) Good idea! (*Wiggles his fingers to show he's ready; ANNABEL "faints" into his arms; he tows her backwards toward the bedroom.*) You'll have to excuse us, folks. (*Exits with her; door shuts.*)

BRONIAN. Come back here, you cowards!

FRIEDA. (*moves toward ALISON*) What's that in her hands? It looks like a note.

BRONIAN. That? Oh, that's nothing. Nothing at all.

FRIEDA. (*plucks it from ALISON's fingers*) Bronian!
Listen to what it *says!*

BRONIAN. I've *heard* it, already.

ANDREW. *I* haven't.

VICKI. What *does* it say?

FRIEDA. It's a suicide note!

BRONIAN. The hell you say!

ANDREW. Let me see that! (*takes note from
FRIEDA, reads*) "I am sorry to be gone like this . . .
but I didn't think Bronian would throw in the towel with
the role . . ."

VICKI. (*accusingly, to BRONIAN*) She trusted you
so! She was counting on that part!

FRIEDA. Oh, the poor child!

BRONIAN. But—!

ANDREW. (*continuing note*) "If I'm going to be
draped in black, which seems suitable to the part I'm
playing . . ."

FRIEDA. A trouper to the end! We *must* arrange for a
black velvet shroud!

ANDREW. (*still on note*) " . . . I want to make sure
it's big enough to suit the temperament of a
churchman."

VICKI. You don't find that kind of genteel modesty in
many modern actresses! Is—Is there any more, Andrew?

ANDREW. (*all choked up, finishes*) Just—"I'll see you
all as soon as possible."

FRIEDA. When we get to that big proscenium in the
sky! Wow, what a story! Give me that note! Where's the
telephone?! (*FRIEDA grabs note from ANDREW,
looks about, agitatedly, but the upstage phone is not
there.*)

BRONIAN. Rory must have unplugged the jack when

he moved the furniture. Do you think a call, right now, is quite—respectful?

FRIEDA. Bronian, I already swamped the opposition today with my radio broadcast. With the suicide-note in my possession, I can write a front-page column that'll be the scoop of the year! (*dashes for bedroom*) Rory! Where the hell did you hide the telephone?! (*exits*)

VICKI. Andrew, I'm so bewildered, I think I'm going to cry!

BRONIAN. I'm going to join you!

ANDREW. Mr. Pendrick, what in blazes has been *happening* here?

BRONIAN. Well, it's really very simple—Charles seems to have given Frieda the impression—(*He halts as FRIEDA pops out of bedroom with phone in her grasp, the jack dangling; door slams behind her as she rushes to plug it in.*)

ANDREW. How's Annabel?

FRIEDA. Rory's giving her mouth-to-mouth resuscitation . . . I think. (*dials furiously*) Oh, if I can only make the evening editions . . . !

BRONIAN. (*pounds on bedroom door*) If you two aren't out here in ten seconds, you're fired! (*RORY and ANNABEL enter, smiling sheepishly; as they pass, he mutters.*) Of all the treacherous—!

FRIEDA. (*on phone*) Hello? . . . *Max!* Get off the line! What do I pay a secretary for?! . . . Well, *find* her! . . .

ANDREW. Somebody please tell me what happened! How did Alison die?

VICKI. (*totally at sea*) It was terribly sudden. She must have been struck by lightning!

BRONIAN. You're overwrought. Please, just accept the

fact that she's dead, for now. Things aren't always as bad as they seem.

VICKI. I hope not. That's the worst embalming job I've ever seen!

FRIEDA. (*on phone*) Ernestine? Grab your shorthand pad. I've got the story of the century!

ANDREW. It used to be the scoop of the year!

BRONIAN. These things have a way of growing. (*to RORY*) Mouth-to-mouth resuscitation! How can you think of canoodling at a time like this?!

ANNABEL. Alison's death was a shock. We were trying to forget.

FRIEDA. (*on phone*) Today, the famous Broadway actress Alison Blair died by her own hand. Cause of death is not yet known, but the tragic note she left behind her speaks for itself—

RORY. Ten-to-one she reads it anyhow!

FRIEDA. It was found clutched in her cold, dead hand in the apartment of famous Broadway producer Bronian Pendrick, and it is he to whom its contents seem to be addressed. . . .

BRONIAN. (*shouts at FRIEDA*) She could have had a fight with her *milkman!* (*pleadingly, to GROUP*) My backers are going to start asking *me* for money!

ANNABEL. Don't be a dope, Bronian! If an actress would *kill* herself when she lost a part in the show, they'll think it's the biggest box office bonanza since *My Fair Lady!*

ANDREW. (*almost in tears, flings a gesture at ALISON*) This is all *my* doing!

BRONIAN. Don't listen to him, Frieda! We *all* helped!

(*FRIEDA—unheard—barely hears him, as she panto-*

*mimes reading of note over phone to ERNESTINE,
during the following dialogue:*)

ANDREW. No, no, the blame is fully upon *my* wretched
shoulders!

VICKI. That's not true! . . . You have *lovely* shou-
ders!

ANDREW. It was supposed to be a joke, a gag! I never
dreamed you'd all take it seriously!

BRONIAN. Gag? What gag? What are you talking
about?

ANDREW. The play! That silly, stupid play I pounded
out last night!

VICKI. Aha! Then you *admit* you're not sick! You *lied*
to me!

ANDREW. *No,* I'm not sick. On the other hand, *you're*
not *Charlotte!*

VICKI. That's different. I said *that* for professional
reasons.

ANDREW. I said I was *sick* for professional reasons!

BRONIAN. Andrew, what about the *play!?* Stop changing the subject!

ANDREW. I crammed that overnight hack-job full of
so many imbecilic goings-on, I was *certain* you'd all see
what a dumb notion you had. I thought you'd laugh at
it, and go back to my original version!

VICKI. But what's that got to do with Alison?

ANDREW. If I hadn't been up all night, *I* wouldn't
have had that run-in with Frieda, *she* wouldn't have
fought with Mr. Pendrick, and *Alison* wouldn't have
done what she did!

(*During next line, FRIEDA hangs up phone, smiling
in triumph, and comes down to join GROUP and
hear what's going on.*)

RORY. When? What *did* Alison do?

ANDREW. She took the news about Bronian's upcoming marriage very badly. She was broken-hearted when she went out that door. I should have guessed what was coming! I should have stopped her!

FRIEDA. If she went out that door, how did she end up on that sofa?

ANNABEL. It was slow-acting poison. She came back to say goodbye before the end.

VICKI. Then it's true! Alison *is* dead! She's been dead all along! That's why she's lying there!

BRONIAN. Why did you *think* she was lying there—tired blood?!

FRIEDA. Charlotte—You mean you saw her alive, just before the end?!

VICKI. Yes. At the time, I thought she wasn't making sense.

FRIEDA. Quick! What did she say?! This may be a *double* scoop!

VICKI. Something about a marquee—with her name up there as "The Late Alison Blair". Annabel *said* she'd be appearing as a prop!

ANDREW. A *prop?!*

ANNABEL. Don't look at *me—you're* the one who wanted real carrion!

FRIEDA. *This is monstrous!* I never heard anything so ghoulish in my life!

RORY. It was Alison's last request.

FRIEDA. To appear as a bowl of carrion?!

BRONIAN. Well—"The show must go on!" Alison appears as carrion. And you get two scoops!

VICKI. Oh, but Miss Nebcott—The cruelest irony of all is that she *hadn't* lost the part! It was supposed to *look* that way so—

BRONIAN. Don't listen to her! She's crazed with grief!

RORY. (*sweeps VICKI up into his arms*) You'd better lie down, Miss! (*starts for bedroom*)

VICKI. Let go of me! What do you think you're doing?

ANDREW. (*grappling with RORY for VICKI*) You put her down!

(*As they struggle, CHARLES enters from corridor with large cardboard box, stops just inside room, staring at the frenzied activity.*)

ANNABEL. (*rushing to assist RORY*) You keep out of this, Andrew. He knows what he's doing!

ANDREW. Well, he's not doing it with Vicki!

FRIEDA. Who's Vicki?

BRONIAN. The girl Rory's not *doing* it with, of course.

FRIEDA. But why bring her name up at *all?*

VICKI. Andrew, have you forgotten I'm Charlotte Carstairs?

ANDREW. What *is* this Charlotte Carstairs routine, anyhow?!

FRIEDA. Bronian, what does he mean?

(*CHARLES, fascinated by activity, goes up, places box on dinette table, takes a script, comes down slowly, studying GROUP of struggling people and paging through the script in bewilderment, during:*)

ANNABEL. Come into the bedroom, Andrew, and I'll explain everything.

VICKI. Rory, will you put me down?!

CHARLES. Hold it! Please! (*Others stop, turn, see him.*) I can't find the place. Which scene *is* this?

FRIEDA. Charles thank heaven you're here! Can *you* tell me how Alison died?

CHARLES. *Died?* I didn't even know she was sick!

FRIEDA. But you're the one who *told* me she was dead, in the first place! Remember? Bronian and the undertaker?

CHARLES. (*sees ALISON*) Is that—? Is she—? You mean—? Bronian! How did *you* know she was going to die?

BRONIAN. I *didn't!*

FRIEDA. Charles, how do you know he *knew?!*

CHARLES. He must have. He took the undertaker over there while she was still alive.

FRIEDA. Bronian! You knew about the suicide! And you didn't stop her!

ANDREW. Why, you dirty rat! That's no better than outright murder!

VICKI. Andrew, wait! *I'm* that undertaker!

FRIEDA. Good heavens! You're *all* in on it! You planned it! You all (*backs upstage from GROUP*) plotted it out, put the idea into her head, drove her to it! But why? Why?!

BRONIAN. Because—Because I love you, Frieda!

FRIEDA. (*staggered, sits on left arm of sofa*) I don't understand! What do you mean?

BRONIAN. You wanted me, I wanted you. Alison wouldn't hear of it. She was in our way! She was going to make trouble. Everybody knew how I felt about you. They all decided to help. It was easy. She never felt a thing.

FRIEDA. But—this morning—you said—?!

BRONIAN. A sham. All of it! I didn't want you to know what we were planning to do. I didn't want those delicate hands stained with blood, even by proxy!

FRIEDA. (*horrified*) Bronian—I didn't even know you cared!

ANNABEL. Of course you knew. He proposed to you, didn't he?

FRIEDA. No! He didn't! That was all a hoax!

RORY. But the tape-recording—the witnesses—!

FRIEDA. (*terrified, almost babbling*) It was the play! Andrew's play! The *first* version. Bronian was reading it to me, the scene where the grocer proposes to the daughter. I put it on tape, for a joke. But then, this morning, when I realized Andrew had changed the entire plot, I knew that speech would never be in it, would never be heard by an audience. I thought I could force him into marriage with it!

ANDREW. How? We could prove it was in the script by the copyright date.

FRIEDA. That wouldn't mean anything except that Bronian came across a well-worded proposal and decided to use it himself!

VICKI. "Well-worded"?! That proposal was one of the funniest bits in the show!

ANDREW. (*reacts*) *What?!*

BRONIAN. *Funny?* Are you talking about the *earlier* version?

ANDREW. She *can't* be!

VICKI. Of course I am! (*to BRONIAN*) You mean that you, a big-time Broadway pro, can't recognize a comedy when you see one?

CHARLES. You know, I *thought* it was kind of funny I proposed from inside a pickle barrel . . . !

BRONIAN. This is what I get for skipping over the stage directions! Why didn't somebody *tell* me?!

ANNABEL. I was afraid you'd turn the show down and ruin Andrew's chances.

RORY. After all, you've never produced anything but

a comedy in your whole career.

BRONIAN. That's true. Even my *King Lear* left 'em laughing!

FRIEDA. You're as bad as the rest of them! To chitchat about *business!* How *can* you, under the circumstances!?

CHARLES. What circumstances?

VICKI. Don't tell me *you* haven't heard about Alison? It must be all over town by now.

CHARLES. I was shopping. It took longer than I thought. They had to—(*Takes black towel out of box*)—dye it for me, special.

FRIEDA. What's *that?* It looks like a moldy coalsack.

CHARLES. I guess it needs pressing. Maybe I can improve it a bit—(*takes vulture from hassock, sets it on floor, starts smoothing towel on hassock*)

FRIEDA. (*Notices vulture for first time: room was dim when she arrived, and since then she's been distracted by the "corpse", urgent phoning, and somewhat eerie conversation.*) Why do you have a stuffed *vulture* over there . . . ? It can't be for *decorative* purposes!

BRONIAN. It's for the play.

ANDREW. *My* play? There's no stuffed vulture in *either* version.

FRIEDA. (*with increasing uneasiness*) There's something strange going on here . . . I feel it . . . I sense it in all your faces . . . Something wrong, terribly wrong . . . and you all fear my finding out—!

BRONIAN. (*afraid of discovery, and unable to conceal it*) Nonsense! We've all just . . . had a hard day.

RORY. Well, sure. I mean, with Alison and all—!

CHARLES. (*sees ALISON for first time*) What about Alison? What's wrong? Why's she lying so still?

FRIEDA. You really *don't* know! That means—It *wasn't* you on the phone, telling me that Alison was dead!

CHARLES. *Dead?* Is *that* why she's just lying there?

ANNABEL. It's as good a motivation as any.

FRIEDA. That suicide-note! I should have guessed. *Anyone* can forge a distraught person's handwriting!

CHARLES. *I* can't.

FRIEDA. (*rushes to him, clutches his arm*) Of *course* you can't! *You're* the only reasonable person *here!*

ANNABEL. Her mind has snapped.

FRIEDA. (*backing with a bewildered Charles toward foyer, wide-eyed and almost incoherent*) I see it all, now! The forged note . . . the guilty faces . . . that obscene stuffed bird . . . the uneasy glances . . . all that confusing conversation—It's a *murder cult!*

BRONIAN. *What* is?!

VICKI. She thinks *we* are.

ANDREW. Do you mean Alison was—was—?! Vicki, say it's not so!

FRIEDA. "Vicki?" That's not the name she gave me! Who is that woman?

CHARLES. That's Vicki Slomber, the undertaker.

FRIEDA. Undertaker! It all ties in! The group kills the victim, that woman embalms her, and then they get out the vulture and practice their unspeakable rites!

CHARLES. (*shrugs*) Everyone's got *rights!*

FRIEDA. *Rituals,* you idiot! (*She is almost at foyer; BRONIAN, ANNABEL and RORY start gently approaching her.*)

BRONIAN. Now, Frieda-baby, you're just upset . . . Have a drink and relax, and you'll think a bit more clearly—

FRIEDA. (*frenziedly hands note to CHARLES*) Take this. When we get outside, run! Find a policeman! Tell him what's happened.

CHARLES. But I don't *know* what's happened.

FRIEDA. Then just run for it! And don't lose that note, it's vital evidence.

CHARLES. (*looks at note*) But — *I* wrote this note!

FRIEDA. (*recoils from him, backs into room*) You?! Then you're *in* on it? *You're* as guilty as anyone else!

BRONIAN. I *think* you'll find he's even a *little* bit *guiltier!*

ANDREW. I knew it! Charles is the *brains* of the whole operation. No one could be that stupid for real!

CHARLES. *I'm* not so dumb. (*takes small bottle from pocket*) Not many actors would have the foresight to buy anti-nausea pills.

VICKI. What do you need *those* for?

CHARLES. I have to face that bowl of carrion, *somehow!* So I asked the druggist for something strong enough to do the trick.

RORY. Charles — You didn't by any chance tell him *what* trick?

ANDREW. Charles, that was all a gag! The hyena and everything!

CHARLES. The druggist didn't think it was very funny.

BRONIAN. Charles — Did he *ask* you where you were *going?*

RORY. Never mind that — Did you *answer* him?!

(*We hear a distant police SIREN, and it is growing louder by the instant; all freeze, numbly.*)

ANNABEL. . . . I *hope* the building's on fire . . . ?!

FRIEDA. Ha-*ha!* Trapped, all of you! There'll be no escaping, now! (*On terrace, ALISON sits up, listens a second to loudening sirens, then starts down toward GROUP, as yet unnoticed by any of them.*) I'm going to see you all put behind bars!

ALISON. Over my dead body!

FRIEDA. (*gives shriek of terror*) You're alive!

(*She backs, shaken, toward sofa; ANDREW and VICKI see ALISON, leap spasmodically to each other's arms, screaming in terror, and faint in fond embrace to floor.*)

ALISON. Well, you're making enough noise to wake the dead!

FRIEDA. B-but—That note . . . ?!

BRONIAN. All that note says is that Charles went out to buy a black towel!

FRIEDA. It says—What? (*scans note with increasing despair*) Bronian! That *is* what it says! How could I have been such a fool? To think that you—all of you— were some kind of murder-cult!

ALISON. Frieda—How do you know we *aren't?!*

FRIEDA. (*stares, nervously alert*) Wh-what—?

BRONIAN. Yes! Didn't it occur to you that we might have planned all this . . . *just to get you up here in my apartment*—?!

RORY. The broadcast and the newspaper story will demonstrate to the world that you weren't of sound mind, today. You see?

FRIEDA. No, I d-don't see . . . !

ANNABEL. Rory means that everyone will naturally think you committed suicide . . . when they find your body . . . !

FRIEDA. (*backs onto terrace, using sofa as wall between herself and others*) You're . . . you're putting me on! . . .

ALISON. You think that's a sofa, don't you! Well, the push of a button turns it into a pagan altar!

RORY. (*grabs up icebucket*) And we use *this* to catch the blood!

ANNABEL. (*lifts black towel from box*) Of course, we cover your face with *this* before we start!

CHARLES. I'm *dying* to find out what you do with the *vulture!*

FRIEDA. (*mindless with terror*) You're joking! You must be! This is New York City in the Twentieth Century! No matter *what* I did today, *how* many errors I made, the police would *surely* suspect murder when they found my body!

BRONIAN. *Not* if we left it where it would arouse no suspicion—

RORY. Where a dead body looked completely *ordinary*—

ALISON. Like in Central Park!

FRIEDA. No! You won't get away with this—! (*looks about desperately for escape-route*)

ALISON. (*helpfully*) Don't try climbing those artificial vines to the roof!

FRIEDA. (*looks upward to right [i.e.: backside of wall where bar is located], reacts*) Vines—? The vines! (*rushes off right on terrace, out of our view*) I'll expose you all! I'll tell everyone—the police, the newspapers, my radio audience, and—*Aaaaaaaaah!*

(*FRIEDA reappears, about five feet off terrace-level, clinging to artificial vine which has apparently torn partly off wall; her descending arc carries her— screaming all the way—right-to-left across terrace, out over low wall, and past dinette-area window; as her scream finally fades to silence, ALISON gets to* U.L. *end of terrace, looks downward toward left.*)

ALISON. Talk about luck! (*starts back toward OTHERS*) She landed right in the back of a *garbage* truck!

BRONIAN. She ought to feel right at home!

ANDREW. (*sits up, groggy*) What happened? . . . Alison! You *are* alive! (*sees VICKI on floor beside him*) What's going *on* around here, anyways? (*listens a moment; then:*) What do those *sirens* mean? (*Starts trying to lift VICKI from floor; she starts recovering consciousness.*) And *where* is Frieda Nebcott?

ALISON. (*thumb-over-shoulder toward terrace*) Over and out.

RORY. What do we tell the police when they arrive?

VICKI. Police? What police? Why are those sirens coming this way?

BRONIAN. It's a long story. Just to be safe, let's put all the furniture back where it belongs, and practice keeping straight faces while we deny everything.

CHARLES. But, *I* don't know *anything!*

ANNABEL. No argument there!

(*All start replacing furniture, during:*)

BRONIAN. I don't know whether to be happy or not about Frieda.

ALISON. Take my advice. Be happy. *I'm* happy.

BRONIAN. Oh, I'm glad she's no longer in a position to mess up my life, now that nobody will believe her again, but—I hate to lose all those backers I convinced about her integrity.

VICKI. It's a shame. Andrew worked so hard on his play . . . How much would he have made, if it was a success?

ANNABEL. Ten percent of the gross.

RORY. Off the top.

VICKI. How much is that in money?

BRONIAN. In the neighborhood of twenty thousand bucks a week.

VICKI. And all you need is the money to put it on?

ALISON. Why, have you *got* some?

VICKI. Well . . . The average funeral costs about fifteen hundred dollars a throw, and expenses only run a few hundred . . . I've been able to put a little bit aside, over the years.

RORY. *How* little?

VICKI. About two-hundred-fifty thousand dollars. (*All stare at her with new respect, furniture-rearranging forgotten.*)

ANDREW. Vicki, I can't let you *do* it!

BRONIAN. *I* can!

ANDREW. Vicki, you mustn't! I couldn't *ask* you to do such a thing.

VICKI. But Andrew, look at it this way: You wrote that second version in a single night, right? Well, there are three-hundred-sixty-five nights a year, and if you do a show a night, and each show brings in twenty thousand dollars a week —!

ANDREW. Vicki —! Even supposing I *did* knock off hit after hit, I don't see how that would benefit *you* . . . ?

VICKI. You don't? I figured we'd open a joint checking account after we were married . . .

ANDREW. Married? But — You're a nice boss, but I don't love you!

VICKI. Andrew, anybody knows an artist shouldn't marry for love. It takes his mind off his work! I love you, and we've shared so much together back at the mortuary that we'll never lack for conversation, so — How about it? Marry me, and I'll back your show.

ANDREW. How mercenary can a person get?!

BRONIAN. Ask *me*, *I* know.

ANNABEL. Look at it this way, Andrew: You're not losing your freedom, you're marrying an angel!

ANDREW. Do you think a person should take a chance on ruining his whole-life-long over an unhappy choice, just so he can make it in show business?!

ALISON. Doesn't *everybody?*

ANDREW. But "Noblesse Oblige" is a *serious drama,* and *Vicki* thinks it's a *wild farce!* What kind of a marriage would *that* make?!

BRONIAN. All right, *don't* marry her. And you'll spend the rest of your life in Peoria!

ANDREW. (*beat; then, to VICKI*) Kiss me!

(*As they clinch, we hear SCREECH of brakes, and SIREN stops, then FOOTSTEPS pounding up the stairs and along the corridor.*)

ALISON. It's the fuzz!

RORY. And we haven't finished the furniture!

(*A loud knocking begins upon the door in the foyer, mingled with doorbell rings.*)

ANNABEL. The kitchen! Maybe we can beat them to the back elevator!

BRONIAN. It's our only chance! We'll rendezvous at my lawyer's office!

CHARLES. Mr. Pendrick—(*BRONIAN looks his way.*)—does this mean the rehearsal is off?

(*Pounding loudens at apartment door; outside terrace, we hear more SIRENS swelling in approaching volume.*)

BRONIAN. I'm afraid so. It's too noisy to concentrate!

ALISON. Bronian, let's get *out* of here!

VICKI. (*tugging ANDREW's arm*) Come *on!* We'll never find that lawyer's office *without* them!

ANDREW. Vicki, *I* can't run out onto the street in my *pajamas!*

ANNABEL. (*scooping up vulture*) Carry *this!* No one will even *notice* what you're wearing!

(*In order: BRONIAN, ALISON, ANNABEL, RORY, CHARLES, VICKI and ANDREW make their exits through the kitchen doorway, on each one's respective speech.*)

BRONIAN. Come on, Alison, that door won't hold them forever!

ALISON. Can you imagine Frieda's *next* column?! I'm beginning to wish I *had* killed myself!

ANNABEL. Don't *say* that! You're our only evidence that Frieda's off her *nut!*

RORY. How do we sell the cops on the idea that our vulture-bearer's *not?*

CHARLES. *I'll* vouch for Andrew's sanity!

VICKI. You *do,* and I'll found my *own* murder cult! . . . Andrew—We can *still* catch a bus for Peoria—?

ANDREW. (*at doorway, in pajamas, clutching vulture in his arms, pauses in dazed bemusement*) What, quit show biz?! (*As VICKI drags him out, and SIRENS and POUNDING reach peak volume—*)

THE CURTAIN FALLS

1. APARTMENT HALLWAY, FOYER DOOR
2. PIER TABLE, WALL MIRROR
3. KITCHEN
4. DINETTE AREA WITH TABLE, CHAIRS, CAFE-CURTAINED WINDOW, RAISED ON 8" PLATFORM ("x")
5. BALCONY, 4-SECTION ACCORDION DOORS, LOW CONCRETE RAILING, ALSO 8" HIGHER THAN STAGE LEVEL ON PLATFORM ("x")
6. SKY/SKYLINE BACKDROP (CLEARLY VISIBLE BEYOND BALCONY AND DINETTE WINDOW
7. PULL-CORD FOR BALCONY-MASKING DRAPES

8. LIQUOR HIGHBOY-CABINET TOPPED BY RADIO; BAR, BARSTOOLS, PHONE
9. BEDROOM-BATHROOM
10. SOFA, COFFEETABLE
11. ARMCHAIRS, HASSOCK
(DOTTED-LINE ARROWS INDICATE "FLIGHT-PATH" TAKEN BY FRIEDA DURING HER ACT III EXIT VIA THE ARTIFICIAL IVY-VINES)

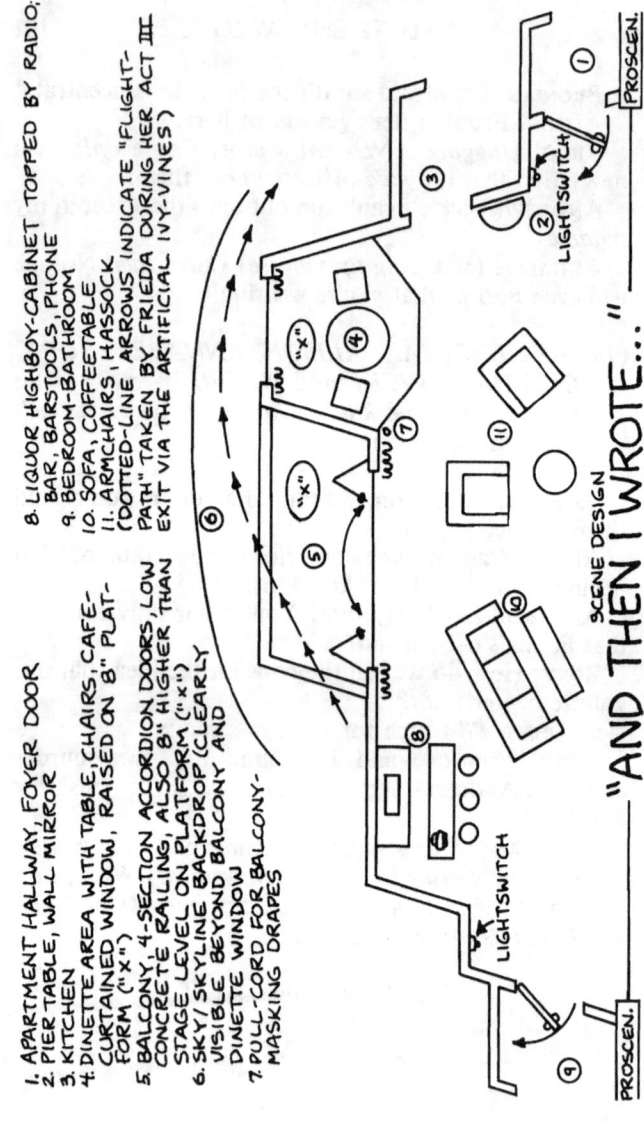

SCENE DESIGN

"AND THEN I WROTE..."

102

www.ingramcontent.com/pod-product-compliance
Lightning Source LLC
Chambersburg PA
CBHW070343120726
47909CB00008B/2724